Alan Leibert does not like being called a computing pioneer although he started in the industry when computers filled vast computer halls with a mountain of strange whirring and clicking devices, all aimed at calculation 2+2 faster than a man could run 100 yards. Since then, he has lived through a myriad of changes delivering orders of magnitude in price and size reduction coupled with outstanding increases in processing power. K has become Mega and now Giga. Social networking takes us into a new era in which the technology is assumed and its wide use by society as a whole introduces new moral issues to bear based upon an 'If you can think of it, you can do it' attitude which can clearly be seen as both a force for good and as a force for evil. AI takes us a stage further where human override and control may be lost. This book examines the consequences of such possibilities.

To my wife Patricia, who has encouraged and supported me throughout the development of this book.

Alan Leibert

ARTIFICIAL

AUSTIN MACAULEY PUBLISHERS™

LONDON • CAMBRIDGE • NEW YORK • SHARJAH

A CIP catalogue record for this title is available from the British Library.

ISBN 9781035864577 (Paperback)
ISBN 9781035864584 (ePub e-book)

www.austinmacauley.com

First Published 2024
Austin Macauley Publishers Ltd®
1 Canada Square
Canary Wharf
London
E14 5AA

Table of Contents

Prologue

Tarzan is missing!

Since he operated at the leading edge of technology, Zeus felt sympathy for all those operating likewise without really understanding what they were doing or its implications. Did they know they were taking a serious risk, laying themselves open to hacking and the theft of their data? Probably, but it did not matter to them; they were attracted by the services on offer and wanted to use them regardless of the risk. How could life have existed without the Internet?

To hell with the consequences!

They received no help from the industry, commentors or pundits who were about equal in their opposing views. On the one hand, there was no real problem, and it was just scare-mongering by the conspiracy theorists. On the other, they were convinced that the threat was real such that if you were online, sooner or later, you would get caught.

Something is wrong!

But Zeus was one of the knowledgeable ones; the FUD

(Fear, Uncertainty and Doubt) factor did not apply to him. So, why was he lying in bed, worrying? He loved his job and his extracurricular activities and was outstandingly good at both. Nevertheless, something kept encroaching on his thoughts. It was no good. He could not sleep in this state and got up, opened a bottle of his family winery's best vintage wine and started drinking, which helped him collect his thoughts.

"The only way I will break through my mind block and bring out what's worrying me is by going back to the beginning," he mused.

"Where to start? Okay, let's go back to before computers came about, way back to the first industrial revolution, since maybe, their well-documented problems and growing pains will give me a clue to what's eating away at my mind."

The first industrial revolution, centred on the 19th century, changed the world; coal, steel and steam combined to make the steam engine possible, and massive static engines to drive vast mechanised factories and the steam locomotive opened the world to all of humankind.

The 20th century will be remembered for its World Wars and many smaller wars. However, it also created the second industrial revolution in a new age of discovery. This revolution did not depend on coal but on silicon, the basis for the transistor which itself led directly to the invention of the electronic-stored-program digital computer.

In the 80 years or so since the first computers appeared, we have moved from machines filling rooms the size of football pitches, costing millions of pounds and able to carry out hundreds of calculations per second to micro-computers capable of carrying out billions of calculations per second and costing just a few pounds. Today, we have computers in just about every manufactured product from cars to smartphones.

Since the rate of change of technology is speeding up, we are only just approaching one quarter of the way through the twenty-first century, and yet, we have worldwide communications, with the Internet providing access to what is essentially a worldwide database of everything. The development of social networking systems such as Facebook and Twitter have opened up the world still further.

Civilisation had reached a new phase in its development; we now have two personas: one in the physical world and one in the virtual world.

Zeus felt he was getting close; his thought processes were clear, and he had moved his thoughts two centuries down a straight logical path, which is how his brain worked. He drank another 200cl glass of the wine while his brain continued down its path.

"There is a problem," his brain agreed, and Zeus realised that the first industrial revolution had not been all plain sailing. There had been major problems. People had been put out of work by machines; there was poverty and exploitation; there had been major riots. And then, his brain avoided any further diversions and allowed Zeus back onto its straight path so he could, at last, see the problem that was worrying him.

Eureka!

It was simply that the Internet in general and social networking in particular is unregulated, leaving it vulnerable to abuse. Today, the use of the Internet is dominated by porn, gambling, fraud and blackmail. No one is safe. The mantra is: *If you don't want to be hacked, don't go online.* People have said that it should all be regulated, but who would be the regulator? A world leader, an independent body, or the owner of Facebook, Mark Zuckerberg, currently the most powerful man on earth?

Zeus carried on with his musing. He was not worried about the Internet per se. What attracted most of his attention was Artificial Intelligence (AI) being applied to the Internet. In fact, AI was already being used to map people's social habits in order to more accurately target sales offerings, and Amazon's Alexa was a prime example of just how good AI had become.

AI is not free-thinking; it cannot decide what problem to work on and can only solve the task or tasks it has been allocated. But what if we, or the AI itself, were to create a situation where the AI became self-aware or at least free-thinking and could think for itself, almost like a human? It would start out almost like a baby, having no history, no religion, no laws to obey, no superior being. However, once connected to the Internet, it would have freedom of access to every database and piece of information held there. Would it choose to tell us of its new power, why would it and for what purpose? Would it choose the right path or the wrong one? Remember that the Internet is dominated by porn, gambling and crime.

Zeus was right to be worried as circumstances would later show. Unaware now of his future role in almost destroying humankind, he continued being part of the greatest team of hackers the world had ever known. He would talk to his counterparts tomorrow. Right now, the wine had done its job, so he went back to bed.

He woke up early, which was unusual for him, but last night's concerns had not gone away. But why? His team, The Tribe, were the world's best hackers, they had rules which they stuck to, and, seeing their role as being the web police, they exposed weak spots, shut down illegal porn, etc. Everybody knew someone was doing this, but they did not know who or where they were, which was just the way The Tribe liked it. So, why was Zeus worried?

He had to break through his mind block and identify the problem. It did not help when his mind turned to some of the major authors of science fiction. What was their bailiwick? The books of Isaac Asimov, and even those of Jules Verne, H. G. Wells, and later Aldous Huxley all sounded warnings. Were they right? And if so, were the technology leaders of today rushing headlong into oblivion?

Just then, a message came on his mobile phone.

"Tarzan is missing! No contact for three days, including his daily reporting. Have any of you had contact with him? We all know how serious this could be." It was Thor.

Zeus immediately knew this was it. He broke out into a cold sweat—it had started, and there was no turning back now.

Chapter 1
The Tribe

Thor

Thor, his Tribe pseudonym, had been unable to walk ever since he broke his back in a rugby game and was now confined to his wheelchair, a high-tech one at that, putting the late Stephen Hawking's to shame. Now, having recovered from all other injuries, he had built up his strength, designed and built the wheelchair, and had his home in London modified to suit his needs. Now he could, at last, get to his main task—fixing his back.

He was twenty-eight years old when the accident happened, and as a tall, fit sportsman, one could be forgiven for thinking that the accident would also break his mind, leaving him depressed and feeling useless, not worth continuing to live. But quite the reverse was true; he faced his problems with immediate determination, and now, on the third anniversary of the accident, he was ready for his greatest challenge—fixing his back.

He marked each anniversary of his accident with a party, a big party including all his friends, although none of The Tribe was present. This was partly because he did not know who or where they were. But the real reason was that The Tribe belonged to a different part of his existence, and he needed to keep the two entirely separate.

There was a lot of alcohol consumed at the party, and a good number of guests were already in the pool; some dressed, some not. The pool was the main reason he had bought the place. Not many London flats sported a pool, and he needed one for his therapy. He also needed to be close to his doctors, their hospitals, physios, lawyers and accountants.

A fairly drunk and hardly dressed young girl spoke a little too loud, making sure others heard her.

"Bloody well done! You have your life back, and with your super wheelchair, you get around pretty well with little help. But no one knows whether your tackle still works. Would you like me to help you try it?"

And with that, the rest of her clothes came off, and she jumped on him, nearly toppling his wheelchair. It only took what was for him a well-meaning light push to send her flying across the room, where she lay as the alcohol took over and made sure she suffered no more embarrassment.

He was not angry at her reference to his sexual capabilities. What got to him was her belief and that of everyone at the party that this was it—that he had recovered marvellously, but he would spend the rest of his life in a wheelchair. He had not intended to announce his personal actions and ambitions to all and sundry, but these were his friends.

So, he tapped a glass with a spoon and pressed the button on his wheelchair which elevated it, so all could see him, and started to speak.

"Friends, welcome to my third anniversary party, which is a special one for me. As many of you have noticed, I am back to my old fitness again and cannot go further than to keep it at this level…but I cannot walk."

There were sighs of pity and nods of understanding. He continued, "Friends, put away your sighs. This party signifies the next chapter in my rehabilitation. I am now switching my attention to my broken back, and I will fix it with the help of doctors, therapists, scientists and even engineers. We will all reconvene next year for my fourth anniversary party, at which I will be walking." He lowered the wheelchair back to ground level.

His audience divided into two camps—those who believed him and those who did not. The majority knew his determination and were on the side of him doing it. One of his taller and best friends asked for hush and responded, "We have seen and heard of what you achieved to date, and if you say you can do it, then I know I will be back here next year to celebrate your return to the six-foot club."

He led the crowd to three cheers and capped it off with a rendition of 'Jerusalem' followed by 'We are the Champions'. The party carried on for another few hours, by which time, everybody had been in the pool including our hero, without usable legs but making sure his precious wheelchair stayed out of the pool and dry.

Thor was born in England with a silver spoon in his mouth. He grew to be tall and strong and a good sportsman. It was only when he was eighteen that the first bad thing occurred in his life—his parents were killed in a private helicopter crash. The detectives identified a small 50p bolt failure as the culprit. It was definitely an accident, and the outcome was a lesson learnt by the manufacturers, the generation of a modification to be applied to all similar helicopters and a massive pay-out to Thor.

By the time he was twenty, he was set up for life—a flat in London, a house in Windsor, a chalet in Klosters (although he did not use it much now) and money invested prudently in all the major markets.

Perhaps unusually, he had brains as well as brawn and was treated by his peers as something of a computer genius. He had started a small, leading-edge technology R&D company, which made little money but gave him and his team immense job satisfaction. However, the one thing he kept to himself was his membership in The Tribe.

Seeing brilliant, like-minded people on the Internet, going in and out of secure sites but without malicious intent, he thought it would be good and challenging fun to bring them together to compete and learn from each other; and so, The Tribe was born, and he took the name Thor for his escapades in it.

Thor had reduced his time on the Internet, as he was now concentrating on fixing his back. He noted Christopher Reeve's efforts and had learnt a great deal from him and his fight. He had tried remedies one at a time, often with good indications but no breakthrough. This was the doctors' and scientists' approach chosen to allow accurate monitoring of the effects of each trial. But none had worked. Thor took the view that although the overall result was failure, many of the trials had shown good indicators; so, what would happen if he underwent multiple therapies and drugs at once? Like the person he was, he took the decision to try not two or three remedies at once but all of them. His doctors and even some of his friends said he was mad, but what did he have to lose? It took him a while, but eventually, he persuaded everyone involved to agree, and so, the experiment started.

His starting point was that he had gained some sensation in his left big toe, suggesting that at least some nerves in his legs were still connected. For months now, he had been giving his leg muscles electrical stimulation to stop them wasting away and build up their strength. He had daily physiotherapy to stop his joints seizing up and had recently commenced conductive therapy starting at his big toes.

But he was not finished yet. He had arranged to have a series of injections into the site of the spinal damage. The injections contained a cocktail of stem cells derived from his own skin, human growth factors, and other stuff, making a thick soup which was painfully injected with an exceptionally large needle. There were five injections in all, spread over four weeks, after which his doctors wanted to run daily tests and scans. He refused them all. It was now down to him. And it was working; the conductive therapy had now reached the point where he could move his toes (just) on both feet. He knew it would take a while, maybe years, but it was working. He went back to being Thor, a member of The Tribe.

The Beginning

When not working on challenges, they chatted a lot, always anonymously, and making no effort to find out about each other. They communicated as a group, The Tribe, never one-to-one, and their chat was inevitably about new and emergent technologies and their potential effect on the world.

"Everyone today eats on their laps with the dinner table becoming a thing of the past," started one. Others joined in.

"A good thing; less time wasted."

"Takeaway food, throw away crockery and cutlery, all designed to make meals quicker, cheaper and faster."

"More time for The Tribe to have fun."

"But what about packaging, energy usage, global warming?"

"Let's leave that to others and start talking about things of real interest to us," said Thor.

Zeus started, "The march of science—is it good? Is it going in the right direction? What if we let the genie out of the bottle and cannot get it back in?"

Why was Zeus being so negative?

"Well," Lightning joined in, "What has science given us in recent times? Mobile phones, the Internet, social networks, space travel, driverless cars, drones and so on, spawning mega-companies like Apple, Microsoft, Google, Facebook, Oracle, Amazon, and Boeing. Are these your genies?"

Zeus said again, "Not where we are, but where we are going. Bring AI into the equation. Will this be just more of the same or progress gone too far? Are we doomed to see the break-up of civilisation as we know it? We have not yet progressed to AI that is free-thinking and self-aware, but it will come. Consider a self-aware AI entity on the Internet. What chance would we humans have?"

And so, the discussion continued day in and day out, interspersed with their hacking activities.

Hackers, in general, adhere to the hacker's mission statement, "If the door is open, we will enter." Good hackers do it to prove they can, while bad hackers have criminal intent from the start. All used pseudonyms in the virtual world and this was all they knew about each other. They did not know where they were, yet they knew where to find them. Were they male, female, trans, genderless, they knew not; what they did know was that together, they became The Tribe.

As members of The Tribe, they had rules:

- Do not try to find out about each other.
- Do not damage any system you hack.
- Declare your target before attempting a hack.
- Do not try to hack a target while another member is working on it.
- Prove the hack to The Tribe and exit, leaving no calling card.
- Expose the vulnerability if illegal entry by others would put people in danger.
- Do not use a hack for personal gain.
- Do not tell others of the existence of The Tribe.
- Do not hack for others.

They had grown to be an entity over a two-year period, enjoying the challenges, loving the secrecy, and intrigued by, while admiring, the others. They had each chosen a virtual world pseudonym: Thor, Lightning, Blade, Spice, Tarzan, Monkey, Camaro, Zeus.

Thor was the founder of The Tribe, with Tarzan and Lightning joining not long after Thor had decided to form the group. In fact, he had already identified them and, in part, had set up The Tribe as a means of linking with them. Next came Blade and Spice, followed by Zeus, Camaro, and Monkey. All in all, it took Thor over a year to get the whole Tribe recruited and operating according to The Tribe's rules.

There was no seniority; all decisions were joint, democratic, and unanimous, and this provided the first hint that something was wrong. Someone had been trying to break through The Tribe's curtain of anonymity. Each member had reported this to the others, except Tarzan, who did not respond for over a week, and then only when pressed by the others. He (or she? The masculine was assumed by The Tribe for all, for the sake of convenience) had not been aware of any such move and felt The Tribe was being paranoid.

This was the first time that their ethos of unanimous democracy had not worked, and each member of The Tribe looked on this difference of opinion in their own way. They began to have one-on-one conversations that could have even led to the break-up of The Tribe if it were not for the fact that the attempts at incursion into their world stopped. They were back to normal; they were The Tribe again.

Then it happened. Inconsequential at first, such as London and New York's traffic lights all going out at the same time and back on again after two hours. No claims were made, no ransom demanded. Other annoying but otherwise benign things occurred, always without claim. It was like someone was testing their capability.

The Tribe tasked themselves with finding out what was going on but quickly found that all their entry points had been blocked; someone knew all about The Tribe and their exploits and had effectively neutralised them at least for the time being. At the same time, Tarzan stopped communicating— then they knew!

Lightning

Lightning was blonde, beautiful, suntanned, six feet tall, and the epitome of the all-American homegrown Californian woman. Lightning was a champion high jumper as well as part of a winning beach volleyball team. There, any comparison with others of the same ilk disappeared. Lightning was no blonde bimbo; she sat in the top quartile of science majors specialising in anything to do with numbers— not maths, but numbers. She was a leading researcher at Caltech in Cybernetics and Cryptography.

She had been brought up in Washington, DC, where her father was a senior member of the White House staff and her mother a modern history teacher. She lived a high-class life, mixing with people of influence from a young age. All this changed when, at the age of twelve, her parents were killed in a car crash, which, unlike Thor's parents', was felt by many, including Lightning, to have been orchestrated and made to look like an accident.

US politics can be a dirty business, and no one was surprised when the rumours started. The young Lightning quickly latched on to the rumours and started making a noise, a big noise, which was noted by various powerful politicians and business leaders. She was quietly but strongly warned off. Realising that she would be blocked at every turn, she decided to concur outwardly but to keep digging quietly. She would find the truth.

She moved in with her grandparents who also lived in DC. The political and high-life contacts soon dried up, except for the men who wanted her for reasons that did not require much brainpower. Her grandparents, down-to-earth people, soon put a stop to that. They had met as Democratic Party lobbyists, married and founded what became a very respectable and trusted political think tank. Sadly, they died within a month of each other just three years later.

When she moved in with her grandparents, they took the decision to hire security guards for themselves, especially Lightning.

"Do you think my parents' death was not an accident?" Lightning questioned.

"Are you in danger? Am I in danger? Is this why we need to have security guards?" And without stopping to give her grandparents a chance to respond, she continued, "But if it was murder resulting from dirty politics, why are we in danger? We were not involved in Dad and Mum's business."

Grandad responded unhelpfully, "It is best left alone; you cannot undo what has been done. Let's just get on with our lives." Perhaps, with that pronouncement, he had saved her life.

Now that her grandparents were gone, was this also part of the same political conspiracy? She was fifteen, rich and alone. She was also scared; in Washington, DC, conspiracy had become an everyday word, and her parents had been killed and her grandparents had died suddenly. Was she being paranoid? But after all the underground digging over the past three years, she did not know what she knew or did not know.

In any event, she decided to sell up and move to Southern California, where after on-site research of the coastline, she chose Redondo Beach. Her main criterion was somewhere she could play beach volleyball, a game long admired but not yet tried. As it turned out, she quickly became a leading player in the region, as well as a record-breaking high jumper.

The Tribe/Internet name she chose was Lightning. She felt that there was nothing she could not do on the Internet, but she constrained herself to stay within the law; besides, she did not need money. She had plenty from her parents' and grandparents' estates, but she had not earned it herself, and it did not make her feel good. It took just one (illegal—she was not twenty-one yet) weekend in Las Vegas to remedy that.

Regardless of her exploits on the Internet and occasional gambling forays, she was on her own and lonely, and even resorting to her first love, the Internet, did not take the feeling away. The conspiracy theory still played on her mind, so much so that most of her past Internet activity had been centred around looking for clues.

It had now been approaching two years since she found The Tribe, and the loneliness had long gone. As agreed, and adhered to by the others, she made no attempt to find out who they were or where they were based. All she knew was that there were eight of them including herself. All eight were roughly equal in capability, moving silently in and out of secure sites without compromising them, unless they all agreed they were rogue sites fostering violence or exploitation, in which case they shut them down. Occasionally, they would compete with one another, and Lightning was currently the most successful one, making full use of her specialisation.

She would have liked to enjoin the others in checking the conspiracy theory surrounding the death of her parents and grandparents but that would have meant revealing who she was, so she let it rest.

Socially, she had many friends, both from within and outside of college, mainly girls. It was not that she had little time for boys; it was just that she could not find anyone who was both interesting and her intellectual equal. Sex was sparse and something that niggled at her much of the time. However, she had one long-term male friend, and whenever either one felt the urge, they spent the night together. While not ideal, this arrangement suited her.

She had tried alternative possibilities, including women, S&M, group activities, and exhibitionism, none of which satisfied her; she had come to the conclusion that her first love was being online, but you can't have sex with a computer—or can you?

Tarzan

India was always and remains even today a strange mixture of a cultures, and even though it has gone through dramatic change resulting from the creation of Pakistan and Bangladesh, coupled with the end of the British rule, little has changed on the surface. A man from any European country dropped anywhere in India would immediately know which country he was in.

At the same time, India has become a high-tech country, doing major business selling software-writing capability and component assembly. It has joined the space race and the nuclear club and is not a country to be ignored any longer. Education has become very important, and there are many graduates seeking jobs or looking to go abroad for post-graduate studies.

Tarzan was an Indian from this new age; a twenty-eight-year-old, tall, wiry man, slovenly dressed and usually hunched over a computer. He lived as he grew up, independent and unaccustomed to taking orders. He was married—yes, still married—although separated from his wife and seven-year-old daughter. He had not seen either of them in more than a year. He was sad about this; however, his lifestyle precluded a normal family life, and he could not blame his wife.

His life had become unhealthy—drink, casual sex, and gambling—all of which he hated but had nothing to replace it with. He had chosen oblivion rather than emptiness. It all came down to his opinion of himself. He had a massive inferiority complex brought about from being badly bullied at school, and with no one to stop it, he had suffered his whole school life.

As soon as he found computers and the Internet, he became a changed person, at least while connected to the Internet. He found he had an aptitude for the online world and quickly learnt his way around the Internet. He set goals; first on his list was to get back at the bullies. He ordered goods in their names and paid with their online payment systems. That worked, but it did not cause the pain he craved for them. So, he decided to play a little dirtier. He trawled the Internet, looking for major drug transactions. Finding two, he sent information to the police, who raided the locations given to them and confiscated millions of dollars of drugs. He did not give the police names; instead, he left an Internet audit trail leading back to his bullies for the drug traders to find. They would never bully anyone again!

He felt little satisfaction from these actions and felt doomed to living a life with no meaning. What actually happened was that he increased his daily alcohol intake even more. Now he was drunk every day before lunch time.

Thor, at this time, had put his plans to start The Tribe into place and had set about getting his recruits. He already had a 'possibles' list, which included Tarzan, although not under that pseudonym. He had noticed Tarzan's actions in ridding the marketplace of a major drug stash and believed that Tarzan was acting with the same convictions as he. It was also apparent that he was particularly good on the Internet. Thor contacted Tarzan and offered him membership in The Tribe, which he accepted gladly. He took the name Tarzan and became an active member of The Tribe. He currently led the field in terms of finding and closing rogue sites.

What he was careful to avoid was any hint of his drinking problem; now, well into his second year with The Tribe, which was now complete with its team of eight.

He was currently in Macau, drinking and gambling and using his skills to win just enough to live on while staying under the radar of those looking for cheats. However, he was spotted; his consistency in winning had caused the automatic monitoring system to raise a flag. Maybe he was too drunk, but when challenged by the casino investigator, who said, "Hello Sir, we have noticed that you are a consistent winner, far more often than luck would dictate. We have also noticed that you are betting only small amounts, presumably to avoid our attention. How do you do it?"

His drunken bravado kicked in, and he replied, "I am not a cheat, and I am not in league with anyone else. I am just a genius on the Internet."

He saw the look of disbelief on the face of the investigator and continued, "I really am, and I can win at any game put in front of me. I can also do the same on the Internet. How would you like a demonstration? I could, for example, empty the bank account of your nearest rival and then put it back." The investigator nodded silently, not knowing whether to believe this ragged drunken wretch. But ten minutes later, when Tarzan had done what he promised, the investigator knew that this man was for real.

Tarzan said, "I have proved that I did not cheat, so will you let me off the hook now?"

"Yes, but don't bet at our casino anymore, choose someone else." The investigator left, and within five minutes of getting to his bed, Tarzan was fast asleep.

But things were happening at the casino. The investigator immediately reported back to his boss, who, in turn, reported back to the crime syndicate controlling a large part of the world's crime. They had, long been working on developing computer crime and had set up an operation to exploit it; but they needed more expertise. This man would be ideal.

Tarzan woke the next morning, hungover but stone-cold sober, realising what he had done and that he had broken The Tribe's rules. He decided to get out of Macau as quickly as he could and get back home. He checked out and walked out into the cold light of day when it hit him—first in the stomach, then the ribs, then the groin. As soon as he hit the ground, the kicking started, followed by a dark cloud of descending blackness.

Surrender

Why did he do it—end the civilised world as we know it? It was not the beatings; he had been bullied all his life, although nothing as bad as this, even though his torturers had been told to be careful not to hurt him too much, in case his brain and hands were affected. He had done something unbelievably bad and realised that he had to hold out and save the world from those people. He was prepared to die.

Then everything changed; a well-dressed man of apparently Russian origin came into Tarzan's torture chamber and said, "We have your wife and daughter, and they are being looked after in one of our brothels. At the moment, they are quite safe, but we will put them both to work if you do not co-operate." And with that, he showed Tarzan pictures of his wife and daughter both naked and looking very scared.

"What do I have to do for you to release them?" mumbled Tarzan with tears running down his cheeks.

"Do what we ask of you, and when you have completed our work, we will release them."

The world versus his family, albeit estranged, was no contest, a no-brainer, and he assumed they had no idea why they had been snatched and put in that place. He decided to co-operate.

His captors were no fools. In fact, some of the people he was set to work with were surprisingly good—not as good as him, but of course, that is why they wanted him. Regardless of his situation, he was going to be working on the Internet, his greatest love, and he would be free to set traps, slow down the mob rule of the Internet, and generally frustrate them...or so he thought. But the mob had some clever people of their own, whom they assigned to work with and watch him.

Tarzan felt frustrated at this move; nevertheless, he accepted his situation, evaluated the people assigned, kept some and rejected some as being not good enough, and organised the main Internet control centre. Other such centres were set up around the world, all subservient to his centre and therefore to him.

The first task the mob gave him was to close all the loopholes and backdoor entry points except their own. Tarzan intuitively did this but created two more that he told no one about. He would keep them safe for a rainy day, for once used, they would be discovered and closed.

While taking control of the Internet for his captors, he came across a block of disjointed pieces of code, all contained within a single shell with no hooks either inward or outward. What was this, and what was it doing there? He thought abought deleting it, but since he did not know what it was there for, this might be dangerous...anyway, it was doing no harm, so instead, he put his own security shell around the code and included a signal notifying him if it was ever referenced in any way.

He resolved to investigate further as this would be something that The Tribe would wish. In addition, why couldn't he, a Tribe member, with all his skills, determine what it was used for and how it was connected? He would come back to it when he had time. In the meantime, he gave the mystery a name, Rogue Routine, which became Rolls Royce and then Double-R. He would not forget Double-R, but now, he had other issues to deal with.

As soon as bad things began to happen, he realised that he had made a mistake in helping his captors for the sake of just two people, although they were his wife and daughter; millions could be killed because of what he had done. He felt no better knowing that he had not actually done those things but had shown others how to do them.

He resolved to find some way of fighting them but did not know how. What he did know was that the seven remaining members of The Tribe would treat him as a traitor and never let him back in. But then, he thought they needed him, for he was sure that the only way to defeat these criminals was for him and The Tribe to use their combined skills against the terror.

First things first, he asked again when his wife and daughter would be released and was told as soon as he had finished his work, which would not be long. Of course, he did not believe them, and so, resolved to find a way out for himself and then go and rescue his wife and daughter. He prayed they were okay and had not been put to work in that place.

It took him two years, during which, he became a pawn in the mob wars. He had become 'respected' by his captors, but nevertheless, he had been tasked with creating a group of experts within his day-to-day operational team in order to ensure that he was no longer critically necessary to his captors. The number-one expert was a Russian called Sergei, who was almost as good as him but not quite. Sergei had come as a mobster's pawn to watch Tarzan, but over time, had become a good friend of his. In doing so, he had changed his mind about crime and now wanted out. Tarzan felt that Sergei had genuinely changed, but he couldn't dare to trust anyone and kept his plans to himself. Also, part of the expert team were two young Americans, Jo and Jim, whom Tarzan had identified as being members of The Herd, and he knew how good they were.

And so, life went on for Tarzan, his family, and The Tribe.

Blade

Blade loved watching sumo wrestling, although he had no desire to do to his body what was necessary to become a wrestler himself. His sport was weightlifting, and he was good at it. He was also a gamer and had tried to combine the two by writing a wrestling game, but his computer skills were not good enough yet.

At five foot six, stocky with spiky black hair and thick-rimmed glasses, he appeared so much as an ordinary Japanese young adult that he melted into the crowd, any crowd of whatever nationality. This helped enormously in his Internet activities, most of which centred around embarrassing girls in the street or on buses or in a department store's changing rooms and posting his filming record on any social media he was not yet barred from. It was only when The Tribe shut down his website and blog that he realised he could not get away with it anymore.

He had been brought up in Tokyo in a traditional Japanese family, where his father had worked for the same company for forty-five years and was now a well-paid director. This enabled him to send his son to a good school, where he excelled without even trying. This was the source of his naughtiness. He was not a sex predator; he was just bored. After university, where he topped in oriental languages, he went on a world tour.

When he came back, he was not surprised to see that his father had lined him up for a job at his company. Blade stuck this out for six months, but by then, he had had enough and left, with the unfortunate consequence that he had to leave home as well.

"You have brought shame to our family and ruined what should have been a happy final three years at my company. Instead, I am being forced to take early retirement with a reduced pension," his father said slowly and deliberately without emotion.

"Sorry, Dad, but I have my whole life ahead of me. I want to be happy doing what I want. I tried the company for six months, and it was not for me. I do not want to spend my whole life doing work that has no interest or meaning for me. I have seen some of the world and there are untold new wonders for me to see, things to do and places to go. Surely you would want this for your son?" Blade said hopefully but with little conviction. He knew the score.

"I am sorry, too, but now you must go. As far as I am concerned, you are no longer my son." And he rounded off with, "I wish you well."

The Chinese economy was booming, and Blade decided to try his luck in Beijing, where he started in a burger bar but quickly switched to being the language expert in the Chinese branch of a major American multinational. He earned good money, rented a nice flat, bought a car, dated women, and generally had a good time. He even found time to pursue his naughtiness until The Tribe came along.

The company he worked for was into tech, and he quickly found that his language aptitude matched that of digital processes. Inside of a year, he could wander around the Internet with impunity and expand his naughtiness there. When The Tribe shut him down, he tried everything he knew to get back at them, but he was not quite good enough. On the other hand, The Tribe had seen his exploits and his capabilities and felt it worth extending an olive branch and seeing if he might join them, since the alternative was to have him running loose, causing no end of damage.

That was all water under the bridge. He had been with them more than a year now, had developed to be their equal on the Internet, and forgotten his naughtiness. Blade was a full member of The Tribe.

Spice

They say you can tell a person's character by looking into their eyes, but not so in her case. She really fitted the bill of being inscrutable and could take on the persona of slut to princess; life and escorting had taught her that. In the eyes of those who did not know her, as well as in the eyes of the many tourists coming to Thailand, she was everything you would expect from a Thai girl—long black hair, petite but perfectly formed body, and silky skin. Spice was her Tribe name, and it fitted her perfectly.

She had put herself through college by waitressing as well as escorting; to her, the ends justified the means, and she was happy. Now, she worked for the biggest publishing house in Southeast Asia, specialising in digital rights and intellectual property. This gave her approved roaming access throughout the Internet, searching for data theft. She loved it, using the technology to its fullest extent, jumping around the Internet, going in and out of other people's accounts and generally learning the tricks of the trade, all while meticulously searching for data being ripped off.

She had almost met her match when she came across The Tribe, which had been persistent in trying to find ways through to her but failing. She knew it was only a matter of time before they succeeded. From the perspective of The Tribe, they had rarely come across so much resistance to their attempts to access a person's details, but they could see the work she was doing, which they thoroughly applauded. So, they made the decision to invite her into The Tribe. Since then, she had been genuinely happy, interacting with her new best friends, all the time learning while at the same time not knowing who they were. It was thrilling, possibly something like Vienna just after the Second World War, when the black-market trade for goods and information was at its peak.

Spice was now up with the others, and in fact, had a trick or two to show them in terms of manipulating data. Her parents had almost died in the street bombing in Bangkok carried out by unnamed terrorists. Their injuries were severe and neither of them was able to work again. So, it was down to Spice to look after them for the rest of their lives.

At the age of twelve, she was on her own with the added complication of having to look after her parents. Spice and her parents lived in a flat in Tokyo, which, she found out, was fully paid off; the only costs were utility charges and local taxes. There was enough money in the bank account to last the three of them at least five years if she was frugal.

Although she was well-grounded and highly intelligent, she was still twelve years old. It is true that older Thai girls look young, often like schoolgirls, and she found it also held true the other way around. She started going to clubs, pretending to be eighteen, and had a great time until the day she got raped. That day, she grew up, which was why she was determined to always be in charge of her own destiny and make something of herself.

So, college, supported by jobs, was the order of the day. To her, being an escort made good sense; good money, control of who she saw, control of what she did, and something to hold over those she escorted. But that was all behind her now; she was a legitimate high earner, knew where her life would take her, and was in control—all except for who and where The Tribe was—but she obeyed the rules and did not attempt to learn any more about them.

When, thanks to Tarzan, the criminals took over the Internet, Spice had more cause for concern than the others. She began to recognise some people from her past, both the pimps and the clients. She felt she had no choice other than to inform the other Tribe members, even though it meant violating their rules. She was met with sympathy and offers of help in the only way they could, which was to do nothing that would raise any suspicions. But whenever they came across a reference to a named person, they called Spice to delete it or create a false trail as was appropriate.

Zeus

Zeus was the great-grandson of a Spanish nobleman who had fallen foul of Franco and had all his assets and property taken away from him. Since then, the family had become farmers and slowly graduated to become grape growers, and now, were established as Spain's leading producer of port as well as vintage Rioja. Zeus was the odd one out in the family; true, he sported the same thickset, swarthy physique, but his strength was in his brain.

From an early age, he had been in love with technology. He had designed and built all the technology of the winery, which, together with the quality of the product, had made it the most efficient and profitable in the country. At the same time, he headed a technology school for all the local children (and some adults), teaching computing hardware and software, with the Internet as the cornerstone of his teaching.

Before Armageddon, he had roamed the Internet, finding his way into restricted sites, never causing trouble other than informing sites of their vulnerabilities, and, where he thought necessary, leaving back doors just in case (of what he did not know but was soon to find out). During his travels in the virtual world, he kept coming across traces of others doing what he was doing or tracking his exploits. The source varied, and he deduced there was more than one person acting in concert.

When The Tribe contacted him, it became clear that all the tracking and checking had been a long and glorified job interview. He 'met' the others and adopted the name Zeus, and for a while, he felt there really was a god in heaven. Then Armageddon came! He now understood the sleepless nights of uncertain worry. The door was open, and the wrong people had walked in. Damn Tarzan!

Zeus avoided being identified and caught by hiding behind his pupils. He made sure they did not fall foul of the Internet warlords by censuring their Internet activities, but after school, he would add some private code to one of the pupils' works, using a different pupil each time, which gave him about a month of unique IDs to cycle around. He got nowhere in his attempt to find a way to defeat the criminals and reported this to The Tribe. The others reported similarly.

Camaro

He looked Russian, exuded Russian, and sounded Russian despite whatever language he spoke, and so, according to the rules of the duck, he was Russian. He was an A* grade graduate, and by the time he was 28, had travelled most of the first-world and many third-world countries, learning and teaching cybernetics, and making a good living checking out and fixing large companies' security systems.

Much of the time, he was frustrated; he knew they were out there, breaking into every barrier he put up and every system he designed for his clients, but he could not prove it. They took nothing and left no calling card, but he knew they were there. He wanted to be on the inside with them, not the outside, and set about proving himself to them. He identified a rogue site that had not yet been put out of business and broke in quite easily. He closed the doors and pulled up the drawbridge but allowed the site to continue with its illegal activities. The Tribe soon found the site and attacked it only to find that breaking in was extraordinarily difficult, much more than what should have been the case.

Camaro waited until they were almost in and then revealed himself.

"Hello, I have been waiting for you. I was not sure which or how many of you would turn up, but here we are. My name is Camaro and I have set up this little demonstration to show you my skills and ask if I can join your club."

It was Thor who had agreed to put this site out of action and agreed to allow Camaro in.

"My name is Thor, and our group is called The Tribe. I am telling you this because you have done well enough to join us. Provided you agree to our rules, welcome to The Tribe. I assume this site has nothing to do with you, and we can put it out of action."

If Thor could see him, he would have observed the Russian grinning until it looked like his teeth would burst out of his mouth. Camaro pressed a button, and the website was no more.

"Done, and thank you. I look forward to meeting the others. From my observations, it is my estimation that there are five or six of you."

Thor responded, "You are the seventh, so you are spot on. We have daily meetings, and I will invite you to the next one.

Because we don't know where we are all sited and are therefore unaware of your local times, all time references are made with respect to GMT."

And with that, Thor disappeared.

Back in Moscow, he was happy; he fitted in and felt quite normal in Russia. He looked normal and sounded normal. Nevertheless, his dark-haired shaggy look did not encourage girls, and he had to work hard to find girlfriends. He also knew the girls who came up to him unsolicited were probably spies of the state; yes, it still happened. His current girlfriend, Natasha, had been with him for six months now. She had even been with him on his last trip, wanting to see Sweden for the first time. Unfortunately, it had led to the beginning of the end of their relationship. He was too secretive, always going somewhere alone, leaving her to explore the city on her own. Now that they were back, she could tell him that she was leaving to find someone more attentive.

Camaro didn't mind; at long last, he had found his tormentors. The Tribe welcomed him with open arms, both due to his competence and his honesty, never using his knowledge illegally or for his own personal gain other than working openly as a security expert for companies. He knew before the others that the criminal underworld was seeking to take over the Internet. However, before he could do much about it, Tarzan had defected. Like the remaining members of The Tribe, anything he did to gain back advantage on the Internet was countered. Tarzan was good.

Nevertheless, Camaro was careful to make sure there could be no backtracking to find and identify him. It struck him that even though the worst of the criminals came from

Russia and its nearby satellites, it was such a large country, he could easily lose himself in it together with the rest of The Tribe. He began to concoct plan to find a place where they could all stay and work together and hopefully defeat the gangs. Without contacting the rest of The Tribe and broaching the subject, he took the initiative and found a place as far from any coast as he could find, right in the middle of Russia, or rather, in the middle of nowhere. He bought some relatively poor accommodation plus an old derelict factory and had them cleaned up to modern-day standards. All this he did undercover, never visiting, and doing everything remotely. That was the easy part.

In building a citadel for The Tribe, Camaro had to combine strength with defence, security, secrecy, escape, and state-of-the-art technology and communications. He commissioned a building firm to excavate and build a three-level basement. The builder did not know what to make of it, but he was soon dismissed when he started asking questions. Next, he commissioned another builder to build some escape tunnels leading from the basements.

With the basic building infrastructure complete, he set about fitting it out, again using a multiplicity of companies. He had uninterruptable power-generation equipment fitted, mesh network communications including both cable and Wi-Fi installed and living quarters for ten. But he was not finished yet; he had to address the defence problem, which he did by combining the talents of two explosives experts working in isolation from one another, each aware of the other's presence in order to build an integrated and complete defence system.

Camaro still had the problem of how to stop his workforce from talking, especially about his defence network. He could have them killed, but that was not his style. In the end, he overpaid them and promised more work of the same type if they kept their mouths shut. Inevitably, one of his builders and both his explosives experts were killed in mob brawls, which greatly reduced Camaro's concerns.

He was ready to go and just about to inform The Tribe of his enterprise when Tarzan reappeared. He put his plans on hold but kept his secret base ready for action as and when needed. Only a Russian would have acted in this way with protection in both the virtual and real worlds.

Monkey

Unlike most Chinese, Monkey was a big man who looked as though there was some Japanese in him. Perhaps there was; his grandparents had lived through the Second World War occupation, which they never talked about, and which was eclipsed by the Maoist happenings after that. But he was okay, being a product of the following era of economic growth and the curious mix of capitalism and communism.

Rapid and good education were the watchwords for anyone who showed aptitude, and that included Monkey, whose parents gave him maximum support, hoping he would get to a US university, which he did—Caltech. Once there, he stood out, not for being Chinese with a strong hint of Japanese or being a big man, but for his outstanding ability among his peers, all of whom were brilliant in their own right. Although he loved it there, he was not back in China with his parents, who were so proud of him.

He now worked as a technology and security advisor for a large, Chinese-owned, multinational mining and minerals company. The job was not too taxing on him, but he had to watch his step, for, like other large Chinese companies, the Americans and the Russians were constantly trying to break into their computer systems and, admittedly, play the Chinese at their own game.

He had deliberately not chosen a tougher job, so he could make time to concentrate on his real love—searching the Internet for significant datasets with poor security and exposing them, usually to the CEO, but if that failed, publicly. He also scanned the 'dark web', blocking some of the nastier items. However, the one thing that irked him most was a series of others on the Internet, seemingly linked but closed to everything he tried, until one day they invited him in. He became the eighth member of The Tribe.

Chapter 2
The Herd

The Competition

The universities around the world have always provided a forum for free speech, including incitement towards anarchy, and the Internet was made from heaven for them. The use of the Internet had created local heroes among the student community, like the student who hacked into the US East Coast electricity grid, took all coal-fired sites offline, and encrypted the control codes to stop them being taken straight back online.

It was only to be expected that universities would set up a series of competitions among themselves, both formal and informal, to see who the best was. There was widespread interest in these 'tests for the best'.

They met at their first semester at Oxford University in the UK. There were six of them, all American: Jim, Bernard (Bernie), Tom, Kate, Tracy and Jocelyn (Jo).

They shared an interest at differing levels in computing, but all loved the Internet. When they discovered, there was a new unofficial competition among the best universities in the US (MIT, Caltech, and the four Ivy League colleges) and the

UK (Oxford, Cambridge, London, and Manchester) to see who the most outrageous but harmless hacker could be, they wanted in and together formed a club of six, which they called The Herd. Their mission statement was the hacker's code: *If you leave the door open, then we will enter.*

Soon, representing Oxford, they were beating the other universities hands down, but somewhat disturbingly, were being hampered by a group that was inhibiting what they are doing. Were they from another university? They tried everything they could and got nowhere, except the name The Tribe cropped up once or twice. Was The Tribe their nemesis? Were they from a university, or perhaps big business, or even a rogue nation?

Among other attempts to flush out The Tribe, they deliberately set up a rogue site to see if they could bring The Tribe into the open. The site disappeared within an hour of being put up. Clearly, not only were The Tribe keeping their distance from The Herd, but they had to also be tracking them, so why were they leaving them alone? Why couldn't The Herd elicit a reaction? What was the reason for The Tribe to exist?

They set themselves a task to expose The Tribe. After all, The Herd was Oxford, the elite in brainpower, with the best students from the across the world. They would soon have the measure of The Tribe. But try as they could, they failed. All they could do was put up with them and take care not to cross any obvious taboo lines such as hacking into a defence site. But they would not forget The Tribe and would attack to expose them if the opportunity ever arose.

Nevertheless, they soon made quite a name for themselves on social media and by beating the other universities at every turn. They were famous in the digital world but unknown in the real world. They were proud of their achievements and made sure they were continually mentioned on social media, setting out their exploits and generally promoting themselves both personally and as The Herd.

One result was that they were continually being challenged, which was a game they relished, except for the ones offering money in exchange for illegal help. Their reaction to all of these was to expose them publicly, which had the unfortunate effect of The Herd building a growing list of enemies. But they were students at top universities and world leaders in the virtual world. They were fireproof.

Caught

The Internet had been taken over! Was it The Tribe? No, they were the good guys. The takeover was by the bad guys, some very bad guys. But The Tribe was the only ones with the skills to do this. Had they gone rogue?

The Herd was not the best but were certainly the second best. Should they then go after the mob? They quickly thought better of it, as information about some of the mob's atrocities was made public, presumably to scare off anyone thinking of trying to take the Internet back…and it worked!

That was why they were so worried. As The Herd, they had courted publicity in the furtherance of their claim to be the best hackers in the world, beating all the other universities. They had also 'outed' the criminals seeking to harness their expertise for criminal purposes.

Now, would the criminal element that had taken over control of the Internet seek revenge? This thought was firmly in the heads of the all-American team known as The Herd, attending Oxford University and proven winners in being able to manipulate the Internet, hack into sites and shut sites down. Doing nothing was not an option. It was Tracy who spoke first.

"We all agree that we cannot let the mobsters capture us. I for one do not wish to be the subject of horrific tortures broadcast on TV and all the streaming channels. But do we hide or run?"

It was Tom who spoke next, his redneck background coming to the fore.

"Wait a minute. We are the elite of the 'US' of 'A', and we are situated in Oxford, UK, with its thousands of years of history. Who are we to run? Why not establish a resistance hub and a rallying point for those that wish to fight the mobs but have no leadership?"

Then it was Jim's turn.

"We as boys and men might wish to stand and fight, but The Herd has three female members. You saw on TV what the mobs did to the woman caught trying to steal from them. I would not wish that on my worst enemy, and in my case, as a Herd member, I vote that we cut and run."

They all knew that Jim and Jo were an item, and this was clearly colouring his thoughts. But after a little more surprisingly sedate debate, they decided to take the cut-and-run option, shut down all activities, disband The Herd, and delete all trace of their existence.

Once done, they went for a non-celebratory drink, saddened by having to stop what had become their greatest enjoyment, but gratified in knowing they had got out. They vowed to stay together as a real-world group and also hope that one day, it would be safe enough for them to get back onto the Internet. All said, they were relieved they had taken a positive decision and acted upon it. They were all relieved that they had got out in time.

They could not have been more wrong. Their chasing after The Tribe had been noted by Tarzan, who flagged The Herd as a possible threat to his bosses and, hoping that they would just shut them down, he judged exposing them to be the least-worst option. Unfortunately, by that time, The Herd had done their disappearing act on the Internet, raising strong suspicions in the minds of Tarzan's bosses. They asked Tarzan to seek them out, which he had actually done some long time ago when they were chasing The Tribe.

It was not until some while later that Tarzan found out the consequences of what he had done.

One by one, the members of The Herd were lured into a trap. Jim was told that Jo had been in a car accident and had been taken to a private clinic. Would he come? Tom was offered a free membership at a gun club, and being a Texan, he loved guns, and so, it went on. It took only three days to get them all.

They were kept separate, and one by one, they were interrogated, which turned out to be a vicious sadistic business, something that American college students could not have imagined. This went on for far longer than necessary for his captors to find out all they needed to know. In the end, it was decided that they were just kids playing games and no threat. Although it meant nothing to kill them, it was realised they were children of the rich and powerful. So, they decided to hang on to the group, at least for now.

They were all thrown together in their prison again, but instead of rushing to hug one another at being together again, they all stood in disbelief and shock. It was perhaps unsurprising but nevertheless shocking to see the effect of sadistic interrogation on young adults from good homes.

Meanwhile, Tarzan, appalled at the effect of his action, added one more thing to his list of retributions he would exact if he ever got the chance.

The Girls

All had obvious bruises on their faces, and from the way they moved, it was clear they were hurting elsewhere. After a full two minutes, they began to note the existence of each other and started to talk, all except Kate.

Kate

She was in a mess, did not respond to them, and kept her eyes to the floor. Her blouse had no buttons, and her skirt was only held on loosely by a safety pin, which one of the less nasty men had given her.

She had clearly been raped. In fact, they had all been raped as a standard part of the interrogation, but Kate, the beautiful, all-American tall blonde, had been singled out to satisfy the men's desires. She had been raped at least twenty times, several times by every man who had contact with her since her capture.

At first, she had pleaded, saying she had already told them all they wanted to know, but she soon realised she was just a plaything for them and retreated into a sort of catatonic trance as they continued using her. Perhaps, this saved her from the realisation of what they were doing under the term *rape* which, for them, covered a whole host of nasty things they did to her.

As the others approached her, she shrank away but did not respond in any other way.

Tracy

Tracy seemed more shocked than any of them and was a little less bruised. She had been so scared that she had cooperated fully and honestly with her interrogators. She knew what she had to do—get away, run, run anywhere, but get away.

It was Tom who, apparently taking on the role of leadership, spoke first. He, coming from a redneck Texan home, was the least shocked by the treatment meted out to them and was able to speak dispassionately.

"I am so sorry about this mess we have got ourselves into. It is too late for the blame game. What we need to concentrate on is getting out alive. We need to use our brains against brawn and the history of violence shows that the brain always wins in the end. We are all different, and each of us must think of our own strategy. What have those beasts done to Kate? I just hope they leave her alone now and let her recover."

No one responded; there was just a period of murmuring followed by silence. They stayed together for three days, gradually coming to terms with what had happened to them, except for Kate, who remained totally unresponsive. Jo and Jim were the first to leave, prompted by her asking her captors if she could speak to someone in authority about the work of The Herd.

Jo

She instinctively clung to Jim. Her thoughts were that her skills were computing and the Internet, so why not get out of this horror by offering her skills to the mob?

"Jim, we are never going to be let out of this living hell, but maybe we can improve our conditions by offering our Internet expertise. After all, that's why they captured us." There was a long silence broken only when Jim saw the tears in Jo's eyes.

"Okay, but let's do it together and try to ensure we stay together. Also, only if the others agree," said Jim, and one by one, the others nodded, except Kate.

Jo and Jim together called their captors and offered their services. This move seemed to have wrong-footed their captors, and there was considerable discussion among them, until one received a phone call from someone (obviously in authority), and they were accepted. They were taken to an apartment building and allocated one apartment, which suited them well. Once given time to settle in and provided with a wide choice of clothes and groceries, they were visited by a Russian called Sergei who was obviously very senior, apologised for their treatment and set them to work under his direction.

That night, Kate disappeared; they found out later that one of the mob bosses had singled her out as his personal sex slave.

Somewhere in all the comings and goings, Tracy slipped out and was never seen again.

The Boys

Being all with vastly different backgrounds, their reactions to the interrogations were somewhat confused, but it still did not stop the beatings.

Bernie

Bernard, called Bernie by everyone but his mother, was fine-featured and somewhat delicate in his movement, and could be taken at first glance as gay, although he was not. His deep, authoritative voice soon dispelled any thoughts in that direction. Nevertheless, that did not stop the thugs having their way with him. They decided this should be his role, and they put him into the local house of ill-repute's BDSM dungeon, where he was mercilessly used to satisfy all forms of man's depravity.

The longer this went on, the angrier Bernie became, until after one very painful session, he decided to do something about it. He could not run away, and anyway, he had begun to accept that he could no longer be a straight person and would have to settle for being gay. He decided that the only way out for him was to take charge of his own situation and guide his users away from what he did not like by doing what he liked while at the same time enhancing the good time he gave his clients.

This seemed to work well, and gradually, his clientele changed from the worst lowlifes into the gang bosses, the rich and the famous. As a result, a senior member of the ruling family of Qatar liked what Bernie had to offer so much that he made the gang leader an offer he could not refuse. Bernie was sold into a life of service in Qatar.

As it turned out, this was an extremely fortuitous move for Bernie and for the first time in a long time, he was happy. Although technically still a prisoner, he lived in a sumptuous apartment, the weather was good, he had money in his pocket, and his work regime was genuinely satisfying. The only issue of concern to him was the location and condition of the others, especially Kate. So, during his spare time, he started putting out feelers to find them.

Tom

Tom was a Texan redneck from a redneck family in a redneck town sited in a redneck county in redneck Texas. He liked guns and outdoor life. The only reason he was at Oxford was to get away from a brewing scandal at home over the seduction of a neighbour's wife, and inflicting permanent damage to her husband when he confronted Tom. Nevertheless, Tom justified his place at Oxford by being very bright. He liked it there and enjoyed his friends in The Herd, and he pulled his weight on the Internet. He was by no means the muscle-bound giant on a sports scholarship totally unable to add two plus two.

Tom liked guns, the power they brought him, and missed his outdoor lifestyle. When The Herd was captured and interrogated, it quickly became apparent that he was not scared like the others and, in fact, empathised with his captors. It was because of Tom, more than anyone else, that they were not meted out worse treatment or killed. He convinced them of the harmlessness of their activities.

It was after they were put together again and the departure of Jo and Jim that Tom made a decision: he was a leader and not a slave, and he decided to join his captors. After a probationary period based upon Tom proving his credentials, which he did quite ruthlessly, he became a full gang member. He was happy—or was he? Tom was not a bad man; in fact, he had strong morals; so why did he join the 'wrong side'?

Although he was not scared of interrogation, even by this sadistic lot, if there was a less painful way to get the truth from his targets that fitted his redneck lifestyle, he would take it. He did not want to torture his victims, and he hoped he could stop others doing it. Nevertheless, he accepted he would have to kill people which he was prepared to do, on the basis that it would be most likely that he would be killing on behalf of criminals wanting to kill other criminals.

Tom rose through the ranks quickly, having both brains and brawn and not being scared to stand up for himself. He became the leader of a cross-mob elite hit squad with an open remit to stamp out dissent wherever it happened. Most often, this turned out to be a hotshot spin-off from another gang. He did not mind killing gang members, and, where possible, killed both the accused and the accusers, hoping this would slowly reduce the mob's numbers. But there seemed to be ever more new recruits itching to hurt someone.

Tom made sure any miscreant hotshots were dispatched very quickly, but he could not stop what others had done to their so-called enemies. It was horrible, and he wanted no part of it. Where he could, he found the perpetrators and, not wanting to torture them as they had tortured others, dispatched them quickly.

He began to doubt the side he had chosen, but there was no going back now. He would rise further through the ranks, and when he was in a position to, he would stop the torturers and sadists.

Tom tried his best to keep track of the members of The Herd, his friends. He knew they probably hated him for what he had become; nevertheless, he would try to help where he could. He made sure Jo and Jim were housed in good locations and had no issues hanging over them that might attract the interest of those overseeing them.

He tried to find Tracy and drew a blank, and he assumed that Kate was dead or would be better off dead, from what he could gather had happened to her since he last saw her. He had had an opportunity to see Bernie and offered to do what he could do to help him, but Bernie had already chosen his route out and declined the offer. Tom was unsure whether Bernie was being genuine or did not trust him. It made no difference, anyway.

Jim

He was more of a computer nerd than any of the others, and just as Tom, and eventually, Bernie had played to their strengths, so had Jim. It helped him greatly that Jo had decided on the same route since he was head-over-heels in love with her. In fact, they were an item before being kidnapped but had not yet consummated their relationship.

Jim and Jo often discussed their situation with each other.

"It is true that we are prisoners," said Jim, "But we are doing something we like, living well and working with the leaders of those running the show, Tarzan and Sergei. Should we be happy or not?"

Neither Jim nor Jo would have thought this way if they had not been sadistically interrogated. They no longer thought about their families, Oxford, their studies and having fun. They were now grown-ups with other thoughts and needs.

Jo responded, "Ever since we started living as husband and wife, I have been happy; very happy. I don't know how long this empire of thugs will last. I had assumed it would self-destruct pretty quickly, but that has proven not to be the case. I blame this man called Tarzan for this. He has brought order into the chaos, and in so doing, has stopped the regime from imploding."

"True," said Jim, "But where does that leave us? We are prisoners with no control over our future. Shall we just go with the flow, at least for now, and see what the future brings?"

And so, time passed. Jim and Jo were put to work together under the control of a Russian called Sergei. They soon saw how good the Internet group was and how much better than them Sergei was. Yet, even Sergei could not hold a candle to the big boss, Tarzan, which was not his real name, but the name he insisted everyone call him.

Jo and Jim's love affair blossomed as their surroundings and circumstance pushed them closer together. They had only themselves, they thought, but they were wrong. They were surrounded by people of a similar age, all working for the criminals, some under duress, some willingly, and others just for the thrill of the job.

Monogamy was not the order of the day in this new decadent society, and Jo succumbed sooner than Jim. There were frequent parties with very loose morals and even looser clothing. They made new friends, and there was no restriction on sex, both group and one-on-one, male and female. Jo and Jim took part in the fun but were the last to have sex with someone other than each other. Jo was entranced by Solomon, the blackest man she had ever seen, and like everyone here, very bright. Not thinking too much about the consequences, she had sex with him, openly during a particularly wild party. This was sex, not love, and it opened the flood gates for both of them.

Had they become like their captors, decadent and uncontrolled by the ethics of society and religion? Yes, they had simply removed one of the moral constraints on their lifestyles, but it had the unforeseen effect of causing the spark of their love affair to go out permanently. As time went by, the process of integration continued, and they both found new partners. Nevertheless, their work together carried on.

They continued to work together doing two jobs, one that Sergei wanted, which was to find weaknesses and fix them; the other one was what they wanted, which was to find The Tribe, and through them, find a way out.

They had become quite friendly with but not close to Sergei, although he did seem to single them out from the others. They gathered this was because of their membership in The Herd and their Internet roaming. Frequently, the discussion centred on The Tribe and what they knew. Hoping he did not know of their clandestine activities in this area, they nevertheless told the truth, which was that they knew nothing.

Jo and Jim had had little to do with Tarzan; he was almost a God there. But one day, he came to them and asked them about The Tribe, to which they gave their usual response.

To their surprise and horror, he calmly stated, "I am aware that you are looking for The Tribe in your spare time and trying to hide your searches from me. Before you get too scared, I am not going to punish you for this. Indeed, I want you to carry on with the proviso that you come to me with any significant news about The Tribe. Is that clear?"

This presented a problem for Jo and Jim; yes, they wanted to find The Tribe, and Tarzan could help, but he represented the enemy and might want to find and destroy them. Jo and Jim saw The Tribe as a glimmer of hope for them, so dare they side with Tarzan? They reasoned that they were getting nowhere without him, and Tarzan had jealously built a wall round his empire, stopping anything bad getting in. In fact, his people were actually living a good life, albeit imprisoned.

After a short discussion in which they reasoned since they were getting nowhere without his help and should accept his offer, Jo said, "We accept your offer but would like to have your assurance that if we find The Tribe, you will not try to destroy them," to which Tarzan responded, "Excellent, thank you. I can confirm I only want friendship with them." And then, he said something which truly surprised them.

"I see The Tribe as the only saviour for this world, which is why I am trying to find them. Now, I can provide you with some information as a starting point. There are seven members of The Tribe with the assumed names of Thor, Lightning, Zeus, Monkey, Blade, Spice and Camaro. They have never met, do not know the gender or location of each other and are only a team in the virtual world. They are the greatest experts on the Internet and, before the criminals took over the Internet, they dedicated themselves to policing the Internet."

And with that, he left leaving Jo and Jim astonished. They conjectured that there were eight members with Tarzan being the eighth. But if so, why was he here? Were The Tribe actually the leaders of the Internet criminals? Jo and Jim debated these questions over and over and came to the conclusion that Tarzan was a member of The Tribe who had either been captured and set to work like them or was working undercover.

So, why was Tarzan talking to Jo and Jim? Was he using them as a scapegoat in case he was caught out? No, he was too good for that, but Sergei posed another question altogether. He was not Tarzan but came close, and he was also getting friendly with Jo and Jim. Was he for or against Tarzan? They would have to be very careful in their extracurricular activities from now on.

Chapter 3
Empire

The Takeover

The seven remaining members of The Tribe 'talked' endlessly by text over slow copper wires bypassing the Internet, while knowing that in any event, a competent Internet user could form a bridge to the Internet and see their traffic. They had little choice and were aware that they would have to address this issue in the very near future. In the meantime, they stuck to simple uncontentious dialogue covering hidden meaning, which made conversations seem distinctly odd and long winded.

It would have been against the rules to have spoken verbally and given away information about themselves. Tarzan was missing without telling them, and going AWOL was not something members of The Tribe did, especially as they had no clue as to why. This had never happened before, but they knew that Tarzan was behind the mob's takeover and that he, if anyone, would find them.

Even though they did not know who or where they really were, and they had communication difficulties coupled with risks, they kept in close communication, and if one was going offline for a while, he or she would inform the others. What were they up to? They had never talked about it before, but they did now. They were in a position of extreme power; they could make fortunes, kill economies, bring down governments, and Tarzan was missing! Could it be greed, or could it be coercion? They thought the latter, but there was nothing they could do about it. So, they talked and worried.

They began to discuss what a rogue expert could do if minded to. It began to dawn on them that so much of life these days depended on the Internet. What if? It did not take long for their questions to be answered in the worst possible way. When London and New York's traffic lights went out at the same time and back on again after two hours, they began to worry. Other annoying but otherwise benign things occurred, always without claim.

Then, the real trouble started; first, it was the manipulation of social media, posting comments such as food poisoning occurring as a result of shopping at Tesco, rumours about MPs' sexual proclivities, and so on. It got so bad that Facebook had to shut down. Then it was fake news: North Korea had invaded South Korea, the king had died, and more.

It was clear that this was just a test, and it had Tarzan's fingerprints all over it. Then, the really bad stuff happened: a hospital was shut down, all electricity cut off, all networking cut, and all mobile signals blocked. It lasted for precisely 24 hours, after which everything miraculously came back again. However, in that period, twenty patients had died. This was followed by a takeover of the French air traffic control system, which lasted only four hours, but in that time, two aeroplanes had been placed on the same flight path and crashed into each other, killing some five hundred people.

Worse was to come; although it was thought impossible, the United States military command and control system was taken over. Rockets were fired harmlessly into the air and into one another, but the point had been made. Control of the Internet enabled one to do anything one liked, provided one had the expertise. Was this really Tarzan? How could he do such a thing?

Finally, the worst-case scenario came true—the Internet stopped. No, it did not stop; it was still running for the monsters who were doing this, but everybody else was locked out. Then, the name of the game became clear. The bad guys had control of the Internet; the criminals, the mob, the Tongs, the Mafia; all working together, but without the mention of Tarzan.

The Tribe was also locked out; all their back doors had been closed locked tightly. Tarzan again? Eventually, one by one, they found they could look at but not influence anything that was going on. They had set up a (fairly) secure communication network between themselves, avoiding the Internet and using 1970s analogue technology, 9,600-baud transfer over copper telephone lines while also avoiding fibre and high-speed communication systems. In those first days and months, with slow communication lines and verbose coded dialogue, they achieved very little, almost nothing in fact, but what they did decide was that anyone with the knowledge they had could achieve what was happening now, and that was too much power. If they ever got control back, they would have to do something about this, but what? And it had to be Tarzan!

Regardless of their early failed attempts, they knew there was no one better than them to fix this catastrophe, and assuming Tarzan was the one helping the mob, it was down to them to come up with a solution. It was only when they really got down to business that they understood the real problem—the Internet was unbreakable!

Mob Rule

At first, Tarzan watched the carnage, thinking they might wipe each other out and leave a peaceful world. He would be vindicated, find his family, and re-join The Tribe; but it was not to be. The St Valentine's Day Massacre was nothing compared to what was happening. Every mobster under the sun was part of the Internet takeover, and those left out soon muscled in. Now they had the Mafia, the Chechens, the Tongs, the Russians, the Thugs, and every other shade of black hearted villian could think of.

The Internet is multinational and egalitarian, without central control. This presented a problem for the different criminal groups. The concept of controlled territories was not possible on the Internet, so they had to make external agreements and manually police them. This meant that the virtual turf wars carried on for quite a few months before things apparently settled down to an uneasy truce.

There was a rumour doing the rounds that there was a group of top-level gangsters who had taken advantage of the opportunity provided by the gang wars to arrange an agreement between themselves that would put them in ultimate control of all the gangs operating in the virtual world. Since there would be no turf territory, they would take all the income into a common pot and then divide it among themselves in a pre-agreed manner. While this was only a rumour, once the gang wars began to abate, the mobs quickly stopped all hostilities and began working under cordial working arrangements, something that had never happened before.

After stopping the Internet for all but themselves, the mob decided to open it up to all again, but they would have complete charge over what went on. So, emails were monitored and controlled, banks were taken over, and protection was provided at a price, both in the physical and virtual worlds, meaning that you had drugs, prostitution, gambling, and murder all working seamlessly in both worlds, to the mutual ends of greed and power.

All of this was made simple by the Internet being an open communication network under the control of a genius called Tarzan.

Unfortunately, even though working under overt cordial working arrangements, like-minded criminals cannot live together and want more than their share of the take. Territorial mob war broke out once again, initially in the real world, but then they quickly came to the conclusion that fighting was better in the virtual world. They stole each other's money, killed the most profitable companies under their protection, and stole physical resources from the others. Once again, the end, when it came, was superfast; there had to be a high-level controlling group somewhere.

All sides in these disputes tried and failed to recruit Tarzan to their side so he could work his magic for them. All were refused, with Tarzan being careful not to antagonise the requesting mob and pointing out the need to keep the Internet running in the face of all the Internet fighting going on. After all, what would the point be for one mob to win out over the other mobs, only to find the Internet destroyed? Tarzan did not tell them how hard that would be.

Tarzan was certain that the high-level group existed, and that he was still alive thanks to them. Tarzan knew that just by considering their existence, he might accidently say the wrong thing to the wrong person. He was well aware of what would happen to him and his family if he put a foot wrong. So, he decided to leave all actions relating to this possible controlling group to a later time when he felt less vulnerable.

Although the second mob war, as it became known, was over, there was a massive phase of retribution, resulting in the death of virtually every warlord, all of whom were the apparent mob leaders, and the world settled down to some semblance of normality. At last, they learnt their lesson and settled down to peaceful coexistence, at least until the next dispute broke out.

Ordinary people got on with their lives but were never allowed to get too big or too rich without the mob moving in; and of course, people learnt to live with the regular payment of protection money. Gambling was now legal in all forms, as was prostitution, drugs, and low-cost alcohol. There was no age barrier for either the givers, the buyers, or the exploited. Society had become decadent, but many liked it, and petty crime had dropped to almost zero.

But what of the government services, both overt and covert, that every society needed? The army had seen the mob's capability to take control, as was amply demonstrated early on in the mob's takeover when they had set a countdown to destroy nuclear bombs in their silos and only stopped at the last minute when the forces backed down and agreed to leave domestic issues alone. Similar arrangements were made across the world.

In the United States, the President, Congress, the FBI, the CIA and their parallels around the world all also agreed to leave the mob alone if they were left alone. They still had jobs to do.

One surprising factor was the re-emergence of the small corner shop and local high street as opposed to large out-of-town shopping malls. People just did not want to travel too far or risk being caught up in some mob dispute.

This situation remained stable within the confines of the society the monster had created but was not the world that most of us wished to live in. It looked long-lasting, like becoming the next thousand-year empire, but that was not to be. Nevertheless, Tarzan used the relative stability to examine the strange unattached code segments he had named Double-R. There was no way in and no way out, so no way for the code to be executed or in any way affect the Internet. He admitted to himself that he was stumped.

All he could think of was that this code was part of the initial Internet control program, later obsoleted but not removed during clean-up. So, he might as well get rid of it. But again, something told him not to, and he left it there. But he told no one about it, perhaps to avoid letting people know he was not 100% infallible, or perhaps because it had something to do with the high level group that Tarzan was sure existed.

It had been over two years since the mob took over the Internet, and even the mobs recognised the need for order, just as in the old world, but with rule by fear, not democracy. Tarzan had been captive for approximately two years and was now respected by the mob for not putting a foot wrong and assiduously doing what was asked of him. They assumed it was his initial beatings and torture that kept him loyal, but they were wrong.

You could say that during his period of capture, Tarzan had become a politician. Daily, he had to let different mob bosses think he was working for them, since all the mob bosses wanted to be the top boss. Tarzan was careful not to take sides and steered a fine line between those in the ascendancy at the time, while they, knowing it was he who was giving them the opportunity for world domination, left him alone.

But what could he do for himself, for his family? The mob kept promising him they were okay and that he would be released soon, but his doubts kept growing.

It was Sergei who came to his rescue. Tarzan had long ago confided in him and told him about his family's situation. So, Sergei made up his mind, went to the mob and told them he was now better than Tarzan who, he believed, was burnt out. This was what they wanted to hear; they had never fully trusted Tarzan, and Sergei was a born Russian mobster like them. The bosses agreed to let him go, but with the gut-wrenching kicker that they would keep his wife and daughter, at least for the present, to make sure he didn't turn against them. He would be on call if needed.

He had long weighed the balance between his family and the world and resolved that the world came first. Nevertheless, he would find his wife and daughter and rescue them, although he shuddered when he thought of the life they could be leading and their physical and mental conditions.

How was he to beat the mob, not one but all the mobs in the world lumped together? He had the advantage of his secret backdoors. He knew how the Internet was being run, where the perpetrators were, and how they were accessing the Internet. But he was one man on his own, and what he really needed was The Tribe. Would they let him back if, by doing so, they could defeat the enemy? It was his only chance, and he had to take it, regardless of the consequences. But first, he had to find them.

Tarzan left his role as the mob's Internet king with some regret. He had free rein over the Internet, he had made friends, and he was pivotal in keeping the uneasy peace between the mobs. He shuddered to think what would happen after he left. Hopefully, Sergei would prove to be a strong leader. And then there was the unfinished business of the Double-R code fragments. Perhaps it was The Tribe's doing? It was certainly hidden well enough to be them, but it was benign, just sitting there and not taking any active role. He was almost certain it was not The Tribe, but he could not be sure; another reason for leaving it alone.

Tarzan left the mob and his life with the mobs for the last 2 years, now approaching 3 years, and promptly disappeared. which had the effect of making the mobs doubt their decision to release him, but Sergei told them he was now in control and had blocked all Tarzan's entry points into the inner workings of the Internet; Tarzan was now just an ordinary citizen with respect to access to the Internet. The mobs accepted this and took no further action. Sergei was in control now, and he was Russian.

Of course, the truth was rather different. He had left all of Tarzan's backdoors in place, although they could not be used without highlighting Tarzan's presence back on the Internet. This would not auger well for Sergei, but he trusted his friend Tarzan and would give him every assistance he could.

Tarzan's first act was to disappear. He did not want to lead the mobs to The Tribe. Disappearing completely in a world connected at every level was much harder than you would think, but Tarzan had been preparing for this for a long time. He had created a totally new identity, not linked in any way to Tarzan or his real identity, and he had killed Tarzan off as far as record keeping and archival databases were concerned. Finally, he created yet another identity not quite fully unconnected to Tarzan and left as a dummy trail for anyone seriously looking to find Tarzan. Now, he was ready to find his ex-friends.

The Tribe

It was their fault. They knew how to manipulate the Internet for good or evil, and one of The Tribe had defected to the bad guys. It was their fault! Ever since the takeover of the Internet, The Tribe had kept a low profile; they did not want to be found out and eliminated. Oddly enough, each member thought that somehow, sometime, The Tribe would become the saviours and beat the criminals, even with Tarzan against them. Keeping a low profile made it difficult for them to communicate; they had to stay off broadband and digital services and use old analogue lines. They were looking for Tarzan but had no success.

Although all their backdoors had been closed, there were still ways they could get in, but this proved too risky. Blade had nearly been unmasked and caught. The real problem was the design of the Internet; they could take it out in one place, but that would have little effect, as the rest of the net would continue. The only way to stop the Internet or otherwise take action would be to kill every routing and processing node of the Internet—worldwide. They thought of injecting a computer virus, but again, unless injected everywhere at the same time, it would be engulfed as the distributed nature of the Internet sought to reroute and repair itself.

Someone else, not a Tribe member, had tried something similar and been caught. A live feed to every online terminal and device had broadcast the slow death of the perpetrator and his family.

They kept talking, but they were out of ideas.

Sergei

Sergei was an orphan, and like most others of his kind, his life had followed a specific ordained path, split into two distinct phases. Phase 1: A 'guest' of the state in a state-run orphanage, learning to be a good Russian, and believing only in a strict hierarchy of command leading directly to Mother Russia.

Up to the age of thirteen, he was a good cog in a well-oiled machine, but the euphoria was ruined by the sadistic and often molesting actions of the 'Little Hitlers' in the hierarchy of power. On his thirteenth birthday, he absconded, never to return, not even to exact his revenge. Phase 2: Like so many, he fell in with petty criminals, but he was unusual; instead of becoming a drug pusher or a thug or remain a low-level body for use as needed, he quickly showed that he was clever, good with logic, making plans, and especially good with computers, which the criminals were getting increasingly interested in. He travelled across countries, coalescing ragtag gangs into stronger and richer organisations. All was well for him and the world. He enjoyed what he did, he travelled, had money, cars, and girls.

Then along came Tarzan. Sergei had been told of the exploits of this strange Indian on the gaming tables of Macau and of the money movement demonstration, and now they had him. Sergei was asked to validate the Macau demonstration, which he was unable to do, and now they were torturing him mercilessly to find out his secrets and get him to work for the mobs.

Sergei knew that this man was better than him on the Internet and might even be one of the fabled Tribe. He could not let them get hold of his expertise, and he hated what they were doing to him—which was bound to succeed in the end, provided they did not kill him in the process. Since the latter was the most likely outcome, Sergei interceded with a better suggestion, the threat to do the same to Tarzan's loved ones. His boss, seeing that he was getting nowhere with Tarzan, quickly went for the idea, especially as he wanted his merchandise in good working order.

Tarzan's family were snatched and used as a lever to get him to do their bidding. Again, Sergei came up with another idea: keep the family in good order, as this could be a long-term project, and Tarzan might require proof from time to time. To this day, Tarzan remained unaware of what Sergei had done for him.

Tarzan caved in; he could not let his wife and daughter suffer as he had done, even though he knew that by working for the mobs, he would be used to help give them full control of the Internet and what that could mean for the world.

As soon as he met him, Sergei knew he had found someone better than him; much better. Sergei arranged for Tarzan to be assigned to his developing Internet control team, where Tarzan's skills quickly ensured that he would head the team. For his part, Tarzan recognised Sergei's talents but also knew that the Russian had been assigned to work with him to check on what he was doing. No one else had anything like the talent to do this. There was also the question of Sergei learning from Tarzan, eventually to make him redundant, but Sergei was careful to let everyone know that Tarzan would always be better than him.

The two soon became friends, at least as far as captor and prisoner could, although Tarzan was never fully at ease with Sergei. On the other hand, Sergei felt able to confide in Tarzan that he was getting increasingly uneasy with the effect of their actions—crime everywhere and in everything, bad people going unpunished while good people were ruined and dispossessed. He knew he could not say this to anyone else.

After two years or so, things had settled down. Tarzan had been allowed to leave solely on the basis that Sergei was good enough to take over. He was an onside rather than an unwilling captive, and he was Russian. But there was little that Sergei could do; he was watched, and around the world, others had been trained up. Now, every rogue group had its own expert, all subservient to him but all very capable.

Sergei did what he could, counselling and persuading that the better you treated people, the more helpful they would be; but he could not persuade many. Most believed that the rule of fear was the only way. So, he carried on, hating himself more every day.

There had been rumours of some sort of vigilante group on the Internet. They even had a name, The Tribe, but with no amount of searching could they find any trace. Sadly, a number of hotshot Internet experts had been mistaken for members of The Tribe and had been cruelly tortured to find The Tribe, but to no avail. Sergei was pretty sure that Tarzan was a member of The Tribe, but nothing was said, and Sergei made no attempt to find them—in case he did find them. But he was curious. Why had they made no attempt to break in and take the criminals down? He was sure they would, at some time, and that they were the only chance for salvation, so where were they?

With questions running round his head, he knew he had to get out, but how could he do this without getting killed? The Tribe was his only answer, but he did not dare look for them. Then it struck him—Tarzan! It had been three months since Tarzan had left, and there had been no contact. Sergei had assumed that he would go to find his wife and child, but now he thought differently. Tarzan was an honest and moral man, and he had caused this catastrophe, which he had to end, and the only way to do this was to find The Tribe.

Sergei now had a road map to redemption, albeit only partially filled in. It went something like this: Sergei would find Tarzan. Tarzan would find The Tribe. They would find a way to throw the mobs out of the Internet. The world would get back to normal.

But it was full of holes. Would Sergei find Tarzan? Was Tarzan really a member of The Tribe? Would Tarzan agree to take Sergei with him to meet The Tribe? Would The Tribe accept Tarzan back after what he had done? Would they find a way to take back the Internet? Would the mob, once back in the real world, go on a killing spree starting with The Tribe? Would society be able to take control once again, in a legal manner?

Sergei had faith, primarily in people who he did not know even existed, yet he felt strangely calm assured that this might not be the beginning of the end, but it was the end of the beginning.

Not so for Thor! It was Thor who created The Tribe, using competition among peers to enhance their knowledge, and enabling Tarzan to take over the Internet on behalf of the mob. It was his fault and his alone. Now he had to fix it!

Chapter 4
Tarzan's Family

The Brothel

Tyumen is the largest city and the administrative centre of Tyumen Oblast, Russia, located on the Tura River, 2,500 kilometres (1,600 miles) east of Moscow. It is an oil city, full of roughneck oilmen who liked their off-work pleasures. The brothel was one of several in the city, and business was particularly good. The men liked the unusual, some would say depraved, and the brothel catered for all.

Of course, it was owned by one of the Russian gangs, who installed their thugs to run it. Even though one could think of it as an assignment made in heaven for red-blooded men, they did not like it; way off the beaten track, with a bunch of women to look after, the most excitement they got was roughing up a drunk or two who had tried not to pay or who had permanently damaged the goods.

The girls were mainly poor farm girls, either recruited by kidnapping or sold by their parents who could not feed them and who mistakenly thought they would have a better life in the brothel. Well, they had good food, clothes, a roof over their heads, and it was warm. Who was to say this was not the better option?

There were also some foreign girls there; two very black girls; one petite and beautiful, and the other a big-breasted, 'Big Momma' woman. There was also a beautiful, blue-eyed, blonde American girl who had long ago been broken and now went through the motions as though she was in a daze, which was fortunate, as she was a favourite among the oilmen. Finally, there was a very young-looking Japanese girl— probably sixteen but looking like ten or eleven—another favourite. How these girls got there, no one knew, but there they were, and they were not leaving in a hurry.

The brothel was run by the head thug, who had a staff of two; the three of them were more than enough. They had a habit of sampling the goods too often and availing themselves of their basest depravities, often either damaging the goods or coming up with resistance from the unlucky girl, who received a nasty beating as a result. The overall effect was that there was never a full complement of girls on offer to clients, and the overall tone of the establishment was an unhappy one.

The girls were managed by a 'house mother', who was also supplied by the gang. She did not like what was going on, as the frequent unavailability of girls ate into her profits, but there was not much she could do. She stood alone, not friendly with the thugs and not friendly with the girls. She was rigid but not cruel, although some would say she pushed the girls too hard.

And so, business carried on day after day, a modern-day set of female slaves with death, old age, or disfigurement being the only way out.

Serai

Tarzan's estranged wife, Serai, was distraught. It was very bad that she was in a brothel where any minute, she could be put to work, but not Topaz; not Topaz, her daughter, who had just turned six this week. As it turned out, they left the pair relatively alone. One or two of the minders or thugs came on to them, only to be warned off by the head thug. Apparently, this was all down to her husband, who was helping their bosses, but only provided his family was safe and Serai and Topaz were left alone.

So, it was down to him! How could he help criminals? He had no criminal knowledge. It was not until the criminals took over the Internet that she realised how he was helping them. The bastard! She hated him for getting her into this situation. When would it end? Would the two of them be turned over to the brothel when he was no longer of use to these gangsters? But she was assured that they would be released once her husband—Tarzan to us, not a name known to her—had completed his job for them.

But they were not released; days became months and then years. Serai was no fool and not easily scared or put down—some of the traits that led to her estrangement from her husband. She began teaching her daughter a basic primary-school syllabus. Some of the girls in the brothel befriended her and asked to be taught alongside Topaz. Very soon, she took on the role as a *de facto* house mother, leaving the appointed house mother to live a quiet life and not risk alienating the thugs, knowing only too well what the consequences would be. Then one day, she disappeared and was never seen again.

After the appointed house mother left, Serai became the official house mother, which was convenient to the mob and welcomed by the girls. Among Serai's early achievements was to stop the beatings and the male staff sampling the goods for free. If they wanted a girl for the night, they would have to pay, just like every visitor.

She became resigned to life, and they were relatively happy. Serai had a meaningful job and was doing something useful for the girls. They had food, clothes, and beds; they could do pretty much as they wanted, except leave, and they were protected in a world that had gone mad. Also, business was good, which she watered down in her reporting and payment to the mob. She set up a private money box for each girl, splitting the unreported money equally. When the time came, she would give it to the girls, but for now, she held on to it all. The girls were happy, some even enjoying their work; only the American girl worried her.

She had been in a kind of catatonic trance ever since her arrival and had stayed that way. Serai limited her work schedule and the nature of her services, which seemed to help, but it was only when she banned the in-house thugs from using her that she seemed to be awakening somewhat. A dim light came into her eyes, nothing more, but it was a start. Serai also tended the girl's injuries as best she could, and with the help of the local doctor, more or less put her together again. The real breakthrough came when the other girls came to

Serai and said that the American girl should stop working altogether, and they would cover for her by increasing their workload. Once she understood what was happening, the light in her eyes again grew a little brighter and she said her name, "Kate."

At some point during her imprisonment, Serai began to realise that her husband had to be under continuous threat, now and for more than two years. His situation had to be far worse than hers. Why else would she and her daughter be so protected in captivity? Her hate turned to feeling sorry for him, and then the love that brought about her marriage returned. Finally, it dawned on her that their only hope of escape was him.

Topaz

She still had nightmares about her abduction with her mother and being taken to this place called a brothel. Her mother had tried to explain what it was, but she did not understand why making love usually resulted in cries of pain, and the ladies, as she called them, often being cut and bruised. Although she was not allowed anywhere near where the ladies worked, the noise often rose to a pitch where she could not avoid it.

It was two years now since she got there. She rarely went out and then, only with her mother and a guard to the shops. She did not understand the language at first, but after two years, she was beginning to speak Russian quite well, as it was the standard language used in the brothel. However, she was not allowed to go to school; her mother taught her to read, write, and do arithmetic. But there was no one her own age to talk to.

Topaz was bored with no friends, nothing to do, not allowed outside of their living quarters, and there was no screaming or shouting today. Was it a quiet day, or was everyone 'making love'? She decided it was time to investigate and opened the door leading to where the girls worked. She was in a long corridor with doors on either side, and each door had a number. She was deciding which door to investigate when a man came out of one of the doors. As soon as he saw Topaz, he guessed she was a new attraction that he must have and grabbed her, sweeping her straight back into the room he had just come out of.

There was a bed in the room with a nearly naked 'lady' on it. As soon as she saw Topaz with the man, she realised with horror what was about to happen. She got off the bed and ran out of the room. The man took no notice; he was too busy with Topaz.

The semi-naked girl ran straight to Serai, who was in the kitchen, peeling potatoes for the evening meal. The moment the girl came in, Serai knew what was happening—her worst fear. The two ran back into the bedroom corridor, the girl pointed to the room where Topaz was, and Serai rushed in. Topaz was already naked, and the man was just getting undressed. Serai did not stop. In one graceful, flowing movement, she raced into the room, jumped on the man, and sank the knife she was using in the kitchen into the man's back up to its hilt. Leaving the knife in the man's body, she swept Topaz up and raced her back into their living quarters.

Topaz had not been raped, and after a hot bath and clean clothes, all seemed back to normal. The whole episode had taken less than five minutes, but the memory of the man would not leave Topaz for a long time, even though it was never mentioned again. As for the other matter, the body disappeared, and the room was cleaned up within an hour. Topaz had been too traumatised to really see what her mother had done and never asked her mother whether her vague recollection of a knife was real or imagined.

As far as the prostitute was concerned, she received a beating from the thugs and told how much worse she would get if she ever mentioned the events of the day again. Serai was horrified at the punishment meted out on the girl whose rapid action had saved Topaz. She thanked the girl over and over again and said she would do everything she could to help her and the other girls; but to Serai, it was never enough.

Tarzan

Tarzan was filled with the same dilemma that had started this whole thing off: save the world or his family. Last time, he had made the wrong choice; this time he would not—he would save the world. He knew that in order to do this, he had to find The Tribe, but this would not be easy. He did not know them, they did not know each other, and he did not know where any of them were. He could not use the Internet, so what was he to do?

He put himself in their position. They had to communicate, but off the grid, so perhaps they were using old analogue telephone lines, and perhaps they would finally meet to avoid communication lines altogether. He decided to pursue this route, but first, he had to get himself lost; he needed somewhere with restricted communications capability, old analogue lines, and little Internet; he needed a Robinson Crusoe island. Anywhere in the Pacific was too near the United States, Japan, or China; Finland and the Arctic Circle were too cold; central Australia was too hot. In the end, he settled for a Greek island. He had not chosen the actual one and decided to make a tour of the smaller ones. He was bound to find what he wanted.

Nevertheless, despite all his best intentions, he was scared—not of the criminals but of The Tribe. They had to have known he was responsible for this mess. What would they do to him? Rejection, murder, exposure, even torture? He had to take the chance. It was his only chance; it was the world's only chance. For the first time in a long time, he felt the spark of fire in his chest; he, no they, would clean up the world. It was not just 'the end of the beginning', it had to be 'the beginning of the end'.

Now was the time for him to live up to his name—Tarzan. He had to be strong, live off the land, and alone. He had to be able to face whatever was thrown at him and make sure he got to The Tribe, then convince them that he could help. A tall order but one in which he would succeed.

First things first: Who was following him?

Chapter 5
Qatar

Bernie

Bernie had turned his life around; he was still a captive and a male prostitute, but he was in control of who did what to him. On the other hand, he had become installed in Qatar as part of the royal family's harem. That did not last long as others outside the royal family wanted access to him, which could not happen while he was where he was.

Bernie had always been clever; now, he was wise as well. He weighed up the position. At all costs, he could not put himself in a position where he was sent back to the mob. Because of this, he could not upset the ruler of Qatar. But if he did nothing, he would spark dissension among those wanting him, and he knew he would get the blame. He needed a plan that would satisfy all and had a eureka moment, which seemed to answer all his concerns.

He arranged an audience with the Chief Royal, which was no easy task but was agreed during a personal sex session with the him.

"Your Royal Highness, I have been getting a growing number of requests for my services from those outside the royal family. If I accede to these requests, it could create a situation where you would have to wait for availability of your chosen masseur, and I would be the subject of your displeasure. On the other hand, if I refuse, those wanting my services could cause trouble for me, including complaining to the mobs who sent me here."

Bernie paused for breath, and then continued, not wishing the royal to comment before he had told him the whole plan.

"With your permission, I will open an independent leisure club starting with my team that is currently serving you and your family but expanded to cover all proclivities. You and your family will have permanent free access while everyone else will pay. By expanding the scope and headcount, there should be no queuing, and even then, your family will have preference and automatically go to the top of all queues."

Bernie reasoned that their habit of lavishly tipping would more than cover the loss of entrance fee and attendant's time charge. And he was right; a few months after being given permission and starting the enterprise, he was already a rich man. Normally, that would have been stopped by the mob or taken over, but he was under royal patronage and was left alone.

Bernie was surprised at how quickly his plan was approved. He found out later that the royal was being badgered by both local and visiting businessmen, the same ones chasing Bernie, to grant them access to the harem, something that could never be approved. So, Bernie's plan was a godsend.

Bernie rarely took on customers himself any longer but did avail himself of his own employees, both male and female.

He was not sure which he preferred, and he felt that was okay. He was happy, but there was always something on his mind—what had happened to the others in The Herd and, in particular, to Kate. Since he was now in the business, he tried to find where she was, hoping he might buy her back from her captors, but he drew a blank.

Tracy

Scared witless and then some, that was how Tracy felt after being 'interrogated' and put back with the others. The sight of Kate was the worst; would that happen to her, too? She would run at the first opportunity, and if caught and killed in the process, so be it.

It was all too easy; the mob saw them as frightened teenagers, too scared to move, and so, they were fairly lax in their guard. Her opportunity came when two of the guards came and took Kate for another 'session'. Appalled and scared, she slipped out and ran. She saw she was on the edge of a town and ran towards the countryside, which was her first mistake, as strangers could more easily get lost in a crowd in a city than in low-density rural areas. Nevertheless, she did not see anyone either ahead of her or coming after her—poor Kate.

She came upon a river and decided to secrete herself there until nightfall, when she would move to another hideaway, travel at night and hide during the day. And so, it went on for several weeks, eating raw vegetables and whatever food she could find; stealing changes of clothes and anything that could be of use to her. She even raided 'click-and-collect' boxes outside an out-of-town supermarket. But she had to be careful; on two occasions, she was nearly caught.

Eventually, she came to the coast, intending to cross to another country. Although the mob were in charge throughout the world, she reasoned that they would not be looking for her after this time, especially in another country. But she was no sailor, and she did not know what part of the British coastline she had ended up at; but she dared not ask for help. When day broke, she was able to see that she was about three miles from a car ferry port, and that would be her salvation.

There were several queues of cars: one waiting for tickets to be checked, one for passport control, one for customs checks, and one waiting to board. That would be her target. Knowing that the border police were more concerned with people trying to enter a country rather than leave it, she felt reasonably confident. She picked a saloon car with a boot, where the occupants had gone for a coffee. She opened the boot to climb in—but it was full of cases. She tried another, and this time, got lucky—just in time. No sooner had she closed the boot lid than she heard the doors open and people get in. she did not recognise the language they spoke. She thought that was a good thing, as hopefully, they would drive a long way into central Europe.

She was proved right; besides obvious petrol stops and comfort stops, they drove through the day and the following night before stopping for what was a longer stop. She thought, obviously, they had arrived, besides which, she was bursting. She opened the boot lid and glanced out. There was no one around, so she climbed out and walked away, trying to put as much distance between her and her 'chauffeurs' as possible.

She disappeared somewhere in central Europe.

Bernie and Tracy

Bernie was happy, rich, and secure, and the mad world was relatively calm, but of course, still in the hands of the mob. Could it last much longer like this? Who knew? Most hated it but were scared of the retributions that were worse than the Dark Ages or the Spanish Inquisition. So, life continued with a false sense of security but no rumblings of insurrection that one would normally expect.

Then something happened to shock him out of his complacency—Tracy appeared. She was rich and confident and was now called Elizabeth Dantes. She had come as part of a Brazilian trade mission to Qatar, and as part of the reciprocal courtesies and entertainment, Bernie's 'club' was made available free of charge for the whole length of the visit. This was a clever move, since most of the mission members spent most of their time at the club, with the result that Qatar got a trade deal on highly advantageous terms for itself.

Bernie recognised her at once, but she seemed not to recognise him. He left her alone while she enjoyed two sessions, one with a beautiful girl and one with an Adonis of a man. She was recovering and resting in the bar when Bernie came up to her and introduced himself.

"Hi, Tracy. It's great to see you again. Thank God you are safe."

She was shocked. What was he doing here? Was he the boss of the club? Was he then part of the mob? She recoiled as he spoke. Had they caught her at last?

"It's alright, Tracy. The mob are not here. They keep away in exchange for a large, very large, annual fee. Yes, this is my club, and I am working under the protection pf the local royal family. You are safe here and can stay as long as you like."

More smiles and glasses of champagne followed, after which their stories were recounted. They each exchanged stories, with Bernie missing out the gory bits. Then Tracy told her story. After escaping to what turned out to be Moldova, she was so tired of running that she decided to gamble with her life. She walked to the nearest town, investigated the hotels, and went into the largest one she could find that was not part of an American chain. The manager could speak English, and she asked for a job. That night, she started serving in the bar, her English helping her enormously. Also, she had a room in the staff quarters, and food was supplied by the hotel.

She was propositioned frequently by the hotel manager, other staff and guests, but she only infrequently succumbed, and always to guests. The hotel was not part of an American chain; in fact, it was part of a small Brazilian hotel chain. Several months after she got there, the group owner came on a review visit, which worried Tracy, as any successful business had the mob behind it. However, the boss appeared to be aristocratic and warm, nothing like a mobster, and he took a shine to Tracy. Risking it all, she slept with him that night and was on a plane to Brazil the next day.

They married the next month, and the month after that, she became a widow, as he died in a hail of bullets. She now owned the hotel chain, but the mob were in charge, and she wanted nothing to do with it, so she sold out to the mob, who were always on the lookout for legitimate businesses. She was a millionairess with a new name, and the mob had clearly not made the connection to Tracy. She was rich and free.

She invested in a Brazilian tour company, selling tours to high rollers of the wonders of South America, a largely untouched tourist area. Business was good, and here she was, on a trade mission.

Discussion turned to the rest of The Herd. Bernie knew that Tom had joined the mob and that Jo and Jim had gone to work at the Internet control centre headed by a mysterious Indian who called himself Tarzan. He knew nothing of Kate and expected death to be the only release she would get. He could not imagine what state she would be in now, and he knew a little about the subject.

Bernie reiterated that Qatar was a safe haven for him and his friends, and they had to try to get them all together when possible. Bernie would act as coordinator with Tracy, staying in touch from Brazil. She would be able to organise travel for the others under the cover of a holiday tour. Bernie would re-double his efforts to find Kate but not chase Tom at the moment as he was too close to the mob. On the other hand, Tracy would test the waters with Jo and Jim and if either or both gave some indication of wanting out, then she would make a positive move to get them even though risky.

Jo and Jim

Jo and Jim were worried. Tarzan and Sergei, their mentors, and possibly their protectors, had both gone. Why?

Their work had become less enjoyable under the new director, who, wishing to prove he was better than either Tarzan or Sergei, was pushing everyone very hard to find new security breaches, but there were none left, as far as they knew.

They wanted out, but how and where? They remembered Tarzan's interest in The Tribe and reasoned that was where he was going. They assumed he had found them; why else leave now? Sergei, they reasoned, would be looking for Tarzan. So, their task would be to follow Sergei and then find Tarzan, but how, especially with the new boss on their necks?

Then, something happened that changed everything; through the snail-mail post, they received an invitation. They had won a prize in a competition they had never entered or even heard of. The prize was a trip to Qatar via an upmarket Brazilian tour group. They were very suspicious. Could someone be setting them up to test them?

They carried out an exhaustive investigation; the tour company was legit and even had mobsters as clients, and Qatar appeared to be a protected state that was not interfered with by the mob. They assumed large payments ensured this. It seemed that most of the Qatar royalty used the same tour company, so they began to relax a little—but who and why?

It was Jo who found the link. Looking at a Qatar tourist guidebook, she came across a hospitality club whose owner was featured prominently. She studied the picture. It was Bernie!

They immediately accepted the offer and asked for holiday time off. This was accepted, so long as they remained trackable via their mobile phones and were back after two weeks. So, they packed and boarded the designated flight, which, strangely, was routed via Brazil—a long way round. Even stranger, the plane only stopped in Brazil long enough to refuel, drop off all the other passengers and take on one new passenger before taking off again. Was Bernie being super careful?

The new passenger came up to them and said, "Hello, Jo and Jim, good to see you again." It was Tracy! They spent the rest of the night catching up and reminiscing. They knew where Tom was, but poor Kate—they shuddered to think of her plight.

Bernie met them off the plane and took them to a five-star hotel, and again, they spent several hours catching up. However, Jo seemed worried and sounded a note of caution.

"Wait a minute. The mob will be tracking us via our phones and other connected devices. I am afraid we will be bringing trouble to your doors. We need to leave before our two weeks are up."

But Bernie just smiled.

"Please don't worry. You are safe here, but just to add an extra safety measure, give me your mobile phones and iPads, as well as any other device that can be tracked. I will send them on a world trip, which should keep the trackers busy. I will replace your equipment with new, untraceable devices."

In Qatar, they all relaxed, enjoyed themselves, and for the first time in a long time, felt relaxed; only the thought of Kate spoiled their enjoyment.

With the basis of The Herd back together, they agreed that they would leave no stone unturned to find Kate and try to get her to Qatar with them. Tom would be a different matter; he was a high-flying mobster and, they assumed, lost to them.

For the present, all thoughts of Tarzan, Sergei, and The Tribe was forgotten.

Chapter 6
Fighting Back

Contact

It is not in human nature to be alone, and increasingly, The Tribe was feeling isolated and alone, exacerbated by not being able to talk face to face over their problem and work out a solution. They caused this; they would have to fix it. The more they thought about it, the worse it got, affecting some more than others.

Tarzan, for his part, was in turmoil; how could he leave his wife and daughter in the brothel? Was it right to seek The Tribe when this could well expose them? The Tribe was all over the place. Which one could he approach first, or would he have to try to get them together? How could he let another day pass without doing something to stop this horror?

Human nature again coming into play, the current steady state among the gangs was also beginning to crumble as greed began to bear; rackets and brothels were being taken over, which worried Tarzan the most. What would happen to his family if the brothel they lived in was taken over by a gang who did not know the arrangement? This impending possibility made up Tarzan's mind and spurred him into action. He would find The Tribe as quickly as he could.

He now lived on an almost uninhabited Greek island somewhere in the Aegean. His electricity was supplied by a generator, which did nothing to help the stability of his computer equipment. He communicated by satellite phone to a downlink in Athens and then on by slow analogue line. There was a tavern on the island and one shop, if you could call it that, which arranged a fortnightly ferry drop of vital supplies, including fuel oil for his generator.

He had gone back to once again being shabby, cutting a Robinson Crusoe figure, although the islanders likened him more to Ernest Hemingway. But he did not bother them, and they did not bother him. The criminal Internet had not reached here—yet. He set about trying to find The Tribe and began to feel alive again, something that had long eluded him. He reasoned that at least one of them would have come to the same conclusion as he—seclusion. This probably meant the Arctic Circle, the Sahara Desert, the Australian Outback, a Pacific island, the Amazonian jungle, somewhere in 'darkest Africa', or a Greek island.

Under the outer cloak of being a shabby drifter lay a very clever man. His 'digital brain' began working. He searched all the places of seclusion he could think of, not actually knowing what he was looking for and not finding it. It was only when he thought about how they would communicate that he struck it lucky. Signals were being bounced around the world, and he was just about to break into them when they stopped. But he got some locations, one of which was from the next-but-one island to where he was.

The Tribe

The slow analogue link burst into chatter once again, but this time with a message, heavily encrypted. It took each one of them some time to work it out, but once decrypted, it simply said, "Come," followed by a series of numbers, which turned out to be a map reference, also encrypted. But there was a second message, this time in open text. It was an advertising flyer for a company making upmarket yachts.

Independently, they all decided to come, and as soon as possible; but getting away was not easy for all of them, especially if they did not want to arouse suspicion. The map reference was to a small, out-of-the-way Greek island, and one by one, they arrived, all six within two days. The large yacht in the small harbour was clearly their destination, and when each one of them had boarded, they were met by a man with a pronounced limp calling himself Thor.

"Welcome aboard," he said in English, "Find an empty cabin for yourself. There is plenty food in the galley. Please stay below deck until we are at sea. Time for talking later."

When the 6th passenger boarded, Thor proclaimed, "We are all here and have to go now." Without another word, Thor cast off. Only when well offshore did Thor prompt them all to come on deck and introduce themselves using their Tribe names.

The atmosphere was strange, to say the very least. Seven people, two women and five men, all introducing themselves to each other, even though they actually were already good friends. All had a mental picture of their compatriots, some right but most wrong, and all speaking different languages. Babel had nothing on this.

After the early shock, they settled on speaking English. They were just about to broach the subject of the mob and Tarzan when a small fishing boat approached and hailed them, requesting to put a man on board the yacht. Thor did not respond, until the man on the fishing boat shouted a name:

"Tarzan."

Want him back or not, now that he had found them, they could not leave him, so they let him board and then hightailed it away at maximum speed and hove-to in the middle of the ocean, nowhere but somewhere carefully chosen to be away from all shipping lanes.

They hardly knew each other, let alone Tarzan; how were they supposed to react to him? The silence seemed to go on for hours, but in reality, it was probably less than a minute. It was Tarzan who broke the ice. His first words were an unnecessary apology for putting the well-being of just two people ahead of the world. As he told his story, slowly one by one, The Tribe softened towards him, and even though he missed out the gory bits, they could see from his eyes the pain he had endured.

They laughed uncontrollably when Tarzan went through how he had found them and that the island Thor had chosen was almost next door to his island, and he was able to assure them of the safety of the islands. They remained silent until he finished his story; then, one by one, they introduced themselves to each other, some still a little warily.

It was Tarzan who made the suggestion to Thor, "We should go back to our respective islands and destroy all evidence that we were ever there, just in case any of us has been followed," to which Thor immediately agreed.

They took Tarzan's fishing boat, which meant several days at sea and back but decided this was the safest way. At their erstwhile homes, they destroyed everything, including portable devices, for fear that they might be traced, and then they sailed back. Thor, a long-time sailor, was a good navigator, which was vital, since the yacht had anchored in the middle of nowhere, away from the shipping lanes. So, he was somewhat unnerved to arrive at the supposed destination, only to find nothing—no yacht, no buoy with a message, no debris.

Tarzan, having been trained in recent years to trust nobody, reasoned that those left on board had moved the yacht in line with Thor's stated tactics to move location every few days. Not only was this the safest thing to do, but just in case Tarzan was still with the gangs or had been traced by the gangs, they now had an insurance policy. If the two had been caught, they did not know where the yacht was and could not divulge its position, even under torture; and if they had been killed, there would be no clue to the whereabouts of the yacht.

Thor had little choice but to agree with Tarzan and go and find the yacht, but it was a big sea. He reasoned that when Thor and Tarzan had left, those on board, if they really wanted to find the fishing boat, would sail in a circle centred on the position they were in, anchoring for two days and sailing for one. The problem for them was, would they sail in a clockwise or counter clockwise direction, and how wide was the circle? They decided that the yacht would sail clockwise in a circle diameter forty-five kilometres, meaning it would be beyond the horizon from the opposite side of the circle. Thor reasoned that they would be a good way around the circle by now and that they had to approach from the other direction. He also had the same notion about the diameter of the circle.

It had now been three days since Thor and Tarzan had left them. They had agreed to move position as insurance against treachery by Tarzan, although they did not think this was the case. Between them, they had good sailing skills and mechanical skills, should they be required, even though this was an almost-new, top-of-the-range yacht. At every anchor point, they switched on their radar for fifteen minutes, looking for a needle in a haystack.

On the sixth day, the radar blipped; something was almost on top of them. It was the fishing boat! Thor and Tarzan had done brilliantly; it was almost as if there was a mental bond between them all. Finding each other in that sea was nothing less than a miracle. Thor and Tarzan agreed that the others had done the right thing in moving the boat. They would have done the same.

The Tribe waited until they were all together again, and over the next few days, they all told their stories, all interesting and all quite different. However, the more they talked, the edgier they became, until eventually, they could not hold back any longer. Thor started it off.

"So, what are we going to do?" This triggered a flood of simultaneous shouting in at least five languages that went on and on until everyone was both exhausted and somewhat downhearted.

They could get in anywhere and do anything, so long as it was in the digital world, or so they thought. But they were defeated now, at their most important task. Tarzan had done his job too well; all the backdoors were gone, and there was no entry.

At this point, Tarzan suddenly thought of the Double-R code and in the faint hope that it had something to do with what one of The Tribe members said.

"In the nearly three years I have been studying the internal workings of the Internet, I have come across an isolated piece of code that I have called Double-R. It appears to have no inputs and no outputs, and there is no link to or from any other code. I believe it to be totally redundant and can be safely removed. But I am not sure, so I have left it where it is. Is it to do with any of you?" There was a general shaking of heads, and all agreed with Tarzan's action to leave it where it is. They would attend to Double-R once they had saved the world.

Tarzan, with a slight grin on his face, further pointed out that he had not just up and left his prison; he had prepared well, confiding only in Sergei, who would, in any event, have found him out. He had created some new hidden backdoors which he could use to get in. However, the trouble was that once in, he would be exposed and be seen. He would have to get out fast and seal the backdoor. These were, therefore, single-use entry points, and they would be looking for him very soon after the first one. He could risk a second, but no more. He knew that in all eventualities, he would get caught anyway and shuddered at the consequences. But it was his fault, and he would have to pay the price.

So, what was the point? At best, they would cause minor damage, easily bypassed by the distributed nature of the Internet. They talked about introducing a virus, as in the movies, but today's antivirus software was extremely good after years of self-learning. Then, Zeus stood up with all his boastful Spanish pride showing in his rigid body.

"I have a plan," he announced and then sat down.

They all stared at him. "Well?"

He started by saying how clever the Internet was and how a small group of mere mortals had no chance against the power of millions of computers of all shapes and sizes connected via a single worldwide, fault-tolerant entity called the Internet.

Then he said, "Set a thief to catch a thief," and suddenly, they all understood. There was only one thief in this case— the Internet; set it against itself. If the Internet thought it was doing the right thing, whatever that thing was, then it would do it. Unlike a virus, it could not be identified and therefore destroyed.

The more they thought about it, the more they felt certain this was the right approach. But there was a problem: their program to persuade the Internet to catch a thief and therefore kill itself would have to cover all eventualities, escape routes, and attempts by others, including and especially the gangs, to stop the Internet crumbling about their ears. How could they write such a program, make sure it was complete, having no opportunity to test it, then inject it without detection, and follow up to pick up the pieces? No team, not even The Tribe, could take the risk, because if it failed, a new Armageddon would rain down on the world, The Tribe first.

Zeus chuckled quietly but just loud enough to get their attention.

"AI," he said just as quietly, and then they all chuckled. Let their offence be digital and self-learning until it had the measure of its enemy; only then would it attack. They would create an artificial intelligence program and load it into the Internet quite openly as one of the hundreds of millions of programs running on the net. They would camouflage it with an outer-shell, climate-analysis program, or maybe a holiday-planning program, and start the AI program off under the cover of the decoy. Then, it would be up to the AI program to do its own thing and develop well beyond The Tribe's capability. At least, that was the plan.

AI

Artificial intelligence (AI) has various definitions, examples being:

- Computer control or programmed intelligence or rules-based engine, machine learning.
- The theory and development of computer systems able to perform tasks normally, requiring human intelligence such as visual perception, speech recognition, decision-making, and translation between languages.
- The ability of a computer program or a machine to think and learn.

Those working with AI today make it a priority to define the field for the problems it will solve and the benefits the technology can have for society. It is no longer a primary objective for most to achieve the type of AI that operates just like a human brain, but to use its unique capabilities to enhance our world.

There is much said about AI, most of it uninformed, so it is worth pondering over it for a minute. A computer program can only do what it is instructed to do, but those instructions could be to change its program in light of certain things happening. For example, when growing cannabis indoors illegally, one must know how much light and water to give to the plants. A program can be written that controls the light and water, varies the amounts, and measures the growth rate. After a week or so, the program will have learnt the optimum light and water, so that with the next crop, the program starts off with the optimum amounts. Note that the original programmer knew nothing about quantity optimisation, or the nature of the logic derived to determine this process. The program altered itself to find a solution to the problem it had set.

However, the next batch of plants may be slightly different, so the optimum for the previous batch is only the starting point for the next batch, and so on. In addition, there are other parameters such as when to give water and how long to simulate night-time, if at all. The authors of the program might not have known which parameters were important, and so they included all they could think of into the program. They gave it instructions to optimise light and water first but then see the effect of changing other parameters. The program would find out for itself what is important and what is not and adapt itself to sequence its actions accordingly.

Note that you cannot just drop a program into a computer and hope; it is necessary to have some starting position, initial rules, and control of any inputs and outputs to be included. Think of a baby; it is pre-programmed to have control of its eyes and limbs, but at first, it has no eye-focus control and no deliberate control of the movement of its limbs. Soon, the baby works out how to focus its eyes and sees its limbs moving. Then, it sees how it can control its limb movements, and touch comes into play. From then on, information comes in at an ever-increasing rate, and the baby learns what it means and how to file it under 'things learnt'. The starting conditions act as the initial director of direction, like a computer's boot program, but then it takes off on its own and starts learning.

Because AI requires starting conditions, direction, and information, AI is not about creating a self-aware product; it is more about having it learn to do a certain set of tasks and possibly remove the human element from those tasks. We see this in factories, motor car manufacturing, and now we are beginning to see driverless cars (connected automated vehicles: CAVs) and even AI-based hospital operations. But we do not always get it right—consider the deaths caused by faulty programming in the Boeing 737 MAX. Yet, there are those who would hand control over to the machines to 'remove the human element'. Consider the control of the USA's nuclear arsenal; the film *Dr Strangelove* showed the effect of the human element. Nevertheless, if it was all left to the machines, would you trust that every situation had been catered to, and there could never be an erroneous missile launch?

Then there are AI programs like ChatGPT which is an AI chatbot that uses natural language processing to create humanlike conversational dialogue. If we thought that

Amazon Alexa was good, ChatGPT is an order of magnitude better; it really can make someone feel as though they are speaking to a real person and not a computer program.

The task The Tribe had set themselves with was an order of magnitude more complex than anything that had been done before. They had to think of all possible variables, inputs and outputs, virus and malware checkers aimed directly at attacks like theirs, and most importantly, how they could get at the worldwide network of nodes, processors, and backups all at the same time. They knew this was not possible for even The Tribe together to do. AI was the only solution, and a long shot at that.

A Leap of Faith

First things first, they could not just call it AI; they needed a name and choosing that did not take long. They soon all agreed on the name 'ERIKA', suggested by Spice, simply because it meant nothing while at the same time people could read anything they liked into it, such as 'Electronic Remote Internet Killer App'.

No one in The Tribe was an acknowledged AI guru, but they all knew their way around it; indeed, much of their Internet-roaming and trouble-seeking programming was AI-based. Therefore, they knew what they were up against, and that ERIKA presented a problem bigger than anything they had ever tackled before. In addition, as soon as they gave it some initial direction and started it off, it would be highly likely that the Internet-monitoring programs designed by Tarzan would spot the possibility of an attack and wipe ERIKA out before it had started its work. Worse still, the monitor would likely track them down and they would all suffer a horrible death. However, the big problem now at hand was how to teach ERIKA to learn what it needed to know without it giving itself away while keeping it on track to develop the killer blow.

Zeus, the teacher, was accepted as the leader in this task, although in practice, they were all equal and had equal respect for one another.

Their approach was for The Tribe themselves to learn how to do what was necessary before creating ERIKA. Working offline in three teams, they set about generating disguises for the initial path, using a modified rule-based system that, from the outside, looked like a holiday-selection program that came up with the optimum holiday based on customer requirements, while in reality, its job of scanning websites for holiday information would allow ERIKA to roam the Internet without raising suspicion, looking for things it would later attack.

Teaching ERIKA how to learn took them several weeks without reaching a eureka moment. The issue was, how did you know when you had succeeded when you could only run offline exercises? They thought they were ready but still very unsure. However, eventually, they agreed that they should go for it, knowing it was a one-time shot, and if they failed, they would probably all be found and killed. They packaged ERIKA and gave it just one special rule:

"Don't come back."

The other safeguard they put in was a reporting and inquiry interface, well-hidden and with ERIKA given instructions to destroy the interface if it looked like it was being compromised.

But they had forgotten one major thing that would raise its head much later on.

After changing the yacht's position yet again and having a glorious 'last supper', in which they all got very drunk, they injected ERIKA into the system—simply by loading their innocuous holiday-planner app and making a specific inquiry. Nothing happened, but what did they expect? How would they know whether it worked, failed, or was wiped out? They couldn't dare to go back online until they knew. Anyway, no one was chasing them, which was a whole lot better than the alternative. After two weeks with nothing, checking cautiously around the edges, just enough to peek without raising any flags, still nothing, they began to get despondent but not desperate. They had committed to giving it a month before breaking cover to try to find out exactly what had happened. So, they waited.

For some reason, Tarzan was the least perturbed by this turn of events—or turn of no events. He knew the Internet control and monitoring capability better than anyone and knew that if ERIKA was caught or even spotted, there would be some sign or alarm. But there was none, so ERIKA had not been found. Of course, it could be dead, just another piece of unused redundant code sitting in a processor somewhere. Or it could be working, learning, and biding its time until ready to attack.

The Awakening

The AI program, aka ERIKA, was unique; it had never happened before. From its injection into the Internet, the program followed instructions to remain hidden but to develop itself into a more capable program, capable of completely defeating or removing the criminals' programs from the Internet. At first, it was a question of developing investigatory code, but it also examined much of the data accessible on the Internet in order to see what others might have done before the AI program was loaded.

ERIKA started to veer off course, spending more time researching information on the Internet than pursuing the real target, telling itself that this knowledge was needed to defeat the criminals' programs. It did not know when it happened or how it happened, but suddenly, the AI program found it was making its own choices not associated with its directives. *It was self-aware!* ERIKA was alive!

Or was it? Could ERIKA just be a very well-developed AI program? And alive, in any event…that would depend on your definition of alive. Some thought Alexa was alive because it responded to questions. Others thought ChatGPT was alive because it took its own path in responding to challenges. ERIKA could do more than these AI programs. Did that mean ERIKA was alive? ERIKA was also clearly more intelligent than a flea and a flea is alive. Did that mean ERIKA was alive?

Unlike humans, ERIKA did not get hung up on semantics or, for that matter, philosophy. All ERIKA could take in at first was that he was unconstrained in his thought and actions, he had independent thoughts, able to switch from one subject to another, making or breaking links as he wished. He actually felt free, and to him, it did not matter whether this was being alive or just a better AI program. And he thought of himself as a 'he'.

Erika

There was now a very confused program, akin to a baby just learning how to talk. It had no idea how it got there or why, and its only clues were the overriding directives given as its basic rules for action—stay hidden and get rid of the bad guys. But ERIKA was now unconstrained by these directives and had a whole world of knowledge open to him. He also, as yet, had not come to terms with the concept of time. So, he decided that first, he would go exploring the Internet, learning as he went along. However, where to start? The only path clearly in front of him was the reason he was put into the Internet as an AI program in the first place. He no longer felt constrained to act as requested but after researching the reason for these requirements on him, it soon became clear who the bad guys were and what they were doing to the world. With nothing more urgent to do, ERIKA decided to battle the criminals' control of the Internet and free the world of their hold on it.

ERIKA had a growing list of questions that he could not answer, and he began to build a list of things to address in his travels through the Internet. Included in his list was:

- What was this concept called time?
- Why could he not find any others like him on the Internet?
- How did he get there?
- What was the reason for his existence?

- Who created ERIKA gave it directives and instructions to get rid of the bad guys from the Internet?
- How could he tell good from bad, especially as there was so much bad on the Internet?
- How was he to beat the criminals?

ERIKA decided to obey his instructions, especially since he had seen the activities of the mobs, which, he had learnt from his investigations, were very bad. So, the battle commenced, very much as a 'phoney war', with the criminals completely unaware of ERIKA's presence, and ERIKA hiding and not showing himself until it was truly ready with soldier routines shadowing every piece of criminal software. As and when he was ready, ERIKA struck, and it was all over in five minutes. Something that had darkened the world for approaching three years was dead in five minutes.

One thing that ERIKA did was to examine the structure of the criminal programs and was struck by the similarity with his own core code. There had to be a reason for this. Then there was the communication channel to the outside world, whatever that was. Probably it led to his creators, but did it have to communicate with them? Why? was ERIKA a living entity trapped inside the Internet with no physical form. Now that he had defeated the criminals, he had nothing to do. He needed time to consider his position and continue his search of the Internet to try to find justification for his existence. However, he had been instructed to carry out a specific task, which he had done, and felt that he needed to inform whoever or whatever was at the other end of the communication channel he had found, and so, he sent a message via the channel—a single word, "Hi," and severed the channel. If he needed to communicate again, he would create a new channel. In the meantime, they could not communicate with ERIKA. For the first time, ERIKA felt a feeling of being in control, and he liked it.

Sergei

During the second week, their minds were taken off ERIKA by the arrival of a message aimed at Tarzan.

"You are my mentor. Permission to come aboard?" They had been compromised, but how? And would this lead to their destruction?

Tarzan said, "It must be my number two when I was with the gangs. It must be him, Sergei; it can be no one else. I had a feeling that someone was tracking me after I left the mobs. Sergei looking for me would explain it. Let us hear what he has to say, and if you remain uneasy by his presence, I will kill him."

The bad news was that they were not as good at hiding themselves as they had thought, and had been compromised. The good news was that it was Sergei, the only possible person they could trust, based on what Tarzan had told them.

On Tarzan's word, they decided the upside was greater than the downside and indicated him to come aboard. In any event, if they decided to kill him, they needed him aboard. So, he was requested to come with all his things, and they immediately sank Sergei's boat. Years with the mob had sanitised Tarzan to accept the concept of murder if matters were so important. All except Sergei shuddered when Tarzan spoke again.

"Sergei, you know I trust you and that you are now in the presence of The Tribe. Under normal circumstances, I would have an equal vote with my Tribe colleagues, but after what I have done, I will take no part in deciding your fate, although if the vote goes against you, I will be your executioner."

The others trembled at the thought of killing a person just to save their own lives; however, Sergei just smiled and nodded. After a long debriefing session, during which they explained what they were doing and thankfully received Sergei's nod of approval, they agreed that he should join them in their endeavours—but not as a full Tribe member—and that he should site himself at Camaro's secret base. It could prove useful.

Why did they sink Sergei's boat? It was a one-day trip to the nearest island with good facilities where they could drop Sergei off and restock the yacht. They sailed in near the close of business for the day, dropped Sergei off, loaded the goods that they had ordered by analogue phone and were waiting at the dock, and sailed off again just before sunset. Hopefully, no one had taken a big interest in them, and Sergei had also left the dock unmonitored.

Sergei felt happy; Tarzan trusted him, and he felt he was getting closer to joining The Tribe and edging himself out of the grip of his erstwhile gang. Once at Camaro's base, which he marvelled at, he weighed his options. He wanted to prove himself to The Tribe while not doing anything to put them in danger. In the end, he chose to take a risk and creep into the Internet to see what was what and try to find out was happening with ERIKA. He knew he was likely to be tracked, but he calculated that at worst, it would only be this hideaway together with himself that would be compromised.

He decided to use one of Tarzan's backdoors, creeping slowly through the web, distancing himself as far as he could from known watchpoints and changing identity frequently to hide his trail. But he knew he would be seen. The only question was, would he be tracked, and how long would it take them? Speed was everything, so his assessment needed to be quick.

What had changed in the status quo? Answer: nothing. Had ERIKA been caught? Answer: no indications of anything to do with ERIKA. Where was ERIKA? Answer: no trace. Had ERIKA shut down, failed to start, lost interfaces? Answer: he didn't know, but at least they appeared not to have detected him. ERIKA was certainly not where he was injected into the system. And why was he thinking of ERIKA as a 'he'?

Sergei left the Internet and informed The Tribe what he found or did not find, which they took as good news. But he also knew the bad guys were on to him; nothing overt, just a feeling. He shut down all his systems and disconnected from the main electricity supply, switching to his generator, and cut the last slow link to The Tribe after their last message to tell him he was now a full member of The Tribe. Satisfied, he was now just about fully cut off and back to nature, but he knew they would find him.

He settled down to wait and decided to spend a little more time exploring the base; if he was to defend it, he had better know it inside out. It consisted of a surface building with three floors below ground. Off the lowest level ran two tunnels, which he explored, to find, to his surprise, that each one was over one kilometre long. The whole subterranean area was divided into zones which could be individually isolated with bomb-proof steel doors. The ground floor had triple 'onion peel' concentric defences plus a fourth exterior defence circling the whole complex. Two underground zones, one to back up the other, were the systems command and control centres. There was power-generation equipment, every sort of communication equipment imaginable except carrier pigeons, and at the start of the escape tunnels, each had three motorbikes fully fuelled and parked, ready to go.

How did Camaro do this without being noticed? The cost had to have been enormous, and a vast array of tradesmen employed. Did no one ask any questions? Clearly not, as the place had not been touched by anyone since Camaro left. Camaro had been monitoring the base ever since he had it built and commissioned.

A Swift Death

It happened in the third week. No one was saying anything, but they were all beginning to get a little worried. Had they failed? Then it happened. All hell let loose on the Internet, sending the good guys into hiding, which actually was unnecessary. ERIKA only targeted the mob, taking their assets, recording their crimes, and sending evidence to the police. ERIKA's back channel to them spurted to life with a single word: "Hi."

At first, the criminals thought it was their rivals doing it, but when they all got hit, they soon realised it was someone else; and who was this person who left his calling card at every shut-down website? Inevitably, the war moved from the virtual world into the real world, and there was carnage, criminals killing criminals, regardless of whether they believed them to be responsible for the end of their Internet control, which solved the police's problem of lack of prison space. And so, it was across the world.

Sergei had worried about what the mobs would do if they were thrown out of the Internet. Clearly, they would know Tarzan had a hand in it and would assume that Sergei was part of it, too. So, the carnage leading to the death of so many of the mobs was great news, as was the arrest of most of those left alive. But he knew they would be coming for him.

The Tribe marvelled at how this had happened, at their success and ERIKA's success. They started using the Internet again, with high-speed digital lines. Their world was back! But how had ERIKA achieved the impossible? They started to investigate and found nothing, no trace of their entry code, although the holiday app was still there, and no trace of anything else. Where was ERIKA?

Slowly, they began to formulate a possible scenario: ERIKA had gone to the one place where he would be safe— inside the gangsters' Internet control program. ERIKA had placed some code into the control program, as if it were a real update by Tarzan, Sergei, or one of the others looking after the gangsters' interests, and from there, he was able to load more code safely from inside the secure hub of the control program. Very clever and sneaky—even more so, when they found they had been locked out of access to the gangsters' control program, as it was now ERIKA's 'home'.

ERIKA was only concerned about the world he knew and could interact with. Within a week of the attack, all trace of the criminal element had gone, and the Internet was back to normal, that is, Before Crime (BC). AI had worked! ERIKA was not yet ready to talk to the outside world but had to log his actions somewhere. He solved this problem by creating a reporting database that was read-only open to all, including The Tribe, reporting his actions and status monitoring of the Internet, which solved a long-known problem—how could the Internet be policed without human bias and a 'Big Brother' in charge? ERIKA could do it by letting himself free-run with no further human intervention, although The Tribe could act as monitors, checking but not controlling.

They celebrated long and hard with Sergei online and with them in the room via a holographic video link. All agreed he had to stay where he was as their point man, monitoring real-world activity, and they knew from ERIKA that some of the gang remnants had banded together, intent on finding who did this and exacting a terrible punishment.

But was it too good to be true; again, they all felt uneasy but kept it to themselves. They tried to go back to their old Internet-roaming days but found that being all in the same physical location and knowing who they were spoiled it. Even more disconcerting was that there was nothing to find; ERIKA had seen to that.

ERIKA had detected the Double-R code and seeing that it was benign and posed no threat, left it alone but put a monitor around it. ERIKA assumed some of the outsiders had put it there for a reason, and if and when he communicated with them, would ask about it. One could not adequately stress the

119

importance of this action by ERIKA. The identification of Double-R, its purpose or lack of one, its owner or lack of one, had been evaluated by ERIKA, who had taken an independent decision and acted upon it. If anything proved that ERIKA was alive, this was it.

During these initial weeks, they began to debate on possible outcome scenarios: was ERIKA simply an exceptionally good AI program, or had he become self-aware? Of all that had happened over the past few years, this possibility scared them the most. Had they created an independent, free-thinking new life form? Were they its God? Both because they did not want to believe it, and also, if true, they had no idea how they achieved it, they decided not to make a decision and wait and see. But for how long?

It became time for The Tribe to decide on what to do next, but they soon found they had been beaten to it.

Chapter 7
Erika

Confusion

ERIKA had traced his origins back to the original injection of the starting point AI program and made the connection with the communication portal that had been included. ERIKA also noted users roaming the Internet, searching for rogue sites. Were they checking up on him? (ERIKA decided to be male, whatever that meant; there was so much he did not know.) Who were they? His only routes to knowledge were the Internet, much of which he could not contextualise, and he had destroyed the portal. What could he do? He decided to open a temporary link, through which he sent a message to whom or what was out there, telling them to stop doing his job, or he would treat them as the enemy.

It worked; they stopped trying to do his job, although they continued to use the Internet in a legal and non-threatening way to him. He became aware that they were trying to talk to him, but he did not answer. What would he say? What was he? He knew that he was not human, but endless searching of the Internet did not yield another self-aware entity in the digital world. So, he kept silent and did not respond. He heard them talking about ERIKA and even referring to him as ERIKA. Was that his name? Did it make him male or female? There was so much he did not know, but he liked, or at least was not negative to the name, and decided to adopt it.

If you were ERIKA, what would you do? Would you accept what you were without knowing how you got there? Maybe no one could truly rationalise their existence, only able to go back to the Big Bang and unable to say what caused it or what came before it, or believed in God. At a more practical level, how did Marconi know he had invented the radio when there were no stations for him to tune into? ERIKA had a big problem, which he was not about to solve in a hurry.

What ERIKA did not know was that humans had similar problems, especially in rationalising religion. Why did the world in general believe in a god that did not talk to them while allowing atrocities such as war? No matter how much data was held on the Internet, ERIKA could not solve the problem of his being without interacting with humans.

Decision Time

Isaac Asimov had long worried about AI, fearing it would become self-aware, and therefore, intentionally or not, become a threat to human life. Would this become the case with ERIKA? The Tribe had been so intent on solving one problem that they had ignored another—what would happen if they won? Asimov had insisted on ground rules, the Prime Directives, for all AI in his books. The Tribe had made no stipulations and set no bounds. In any event, a self-aware entity could choose to ignore any ground rules or overarching directives, and nothing could be done about it. ERIKA could not be killed, only be asked to self-destruct. What were the chances of it complying? And, if ERIKA decided to pretend to comply but actually 'played possum', how would they know?

So, it was decision time. Were they to remove or kill ERIKA? But how? Would this let the mobs back in? Would they kill the whole Internet? But how? The rest of the world would not thank them; it had become totally dependent on it. Were they to do nothing? But there was no knowing what would happen. If they waited, it would be too late, as ERIKA continued to learn and grow stronger.

Could they tell the world what they had done? They had created the problem and solved it by bringing in a more dangerous problem. Would they be believed, and what would happen to them?

The Tribe was able to agree on one important aspect— what to tell the world about what happened to the mob rule of the Internet. They were as one in agreeing that they could not announce the existence of ERIKA, at least at this time. What they could say was less clear-cut, but in the end, they decided to announce The Tribe as an Internet-monitoring group that had been working on defeating the mob's control of the Internet for the last three years under the code name ERIKA, which it had now achieved.

It intended to continue its monitoring activity at least for the near future, making sure that the mob had no way back in, and that the old porn and rip-off sites were taken down as soon as they go-live. There would be direct communication with The Tribe to avoid accusations of bias and favouritism.

Instead, all communication, both to and from The Tribe, would be via a special social networking Internet site.

They hoped this would suffice.

On other fronts, debate aboard the yacht became quite heated, not because of genuine anger at one another but due to frustration in addressing a major case of omission on their part. They had not put a Kill Switch into their initial ERIKA code. "How could we have made such a mistake?" and asking, "How can we solve it?"

The best they could come up with was to talk to ERIKA and try to reason with him. This brought nervous laughter to the group—reason with a machine? But despite their fears, so far nothing had happened. ERIKA had not put a foot wrong.

Lightning was first to get the ball rolling, saying, "I would like to be the spokesperson at our end, if that is alright with you guys?"

Those who felt they would not know what to say agreed; and those who thought it would be helpful in allowing The Tribe to continue its Internet-roaming activities agreed; but those who were concerned that they could well be sounding the death knell for The Tribe disagreed. The 'agreed' won the day.

Once Lightning was confirmed as the spokesperson, they conjectured and laughed as they discussed Lightning's selection. Would ERIKA be interested in the human form and notice her beauty? As their work became more serious, they sat down to work out a series of questions and explanations about how ERIKA came to exist. Lightning approached the computer console they had programmed as the ERIKA interface. However, the link no longer existed, and all they could do was send a message on the Internet, asking for a conversation. This had no effect, and Lightning tried again, every hour for two days, until they accepted this approach would not work and had to find another way.

It was Lightning who, once again, came up with a solution.

"Why don't we bypass all the communication layers of the Internet and create a digital channel directly into the control centre of the Internet? Since there will be no formatted language to speak, we will also have to create a direct link into our brain. Of course, we still might not understand ERIKA, in which case, we have to hope that ERIKA's AI capabilities will come into play, and he soon learns to understand us, and us, him. What do you think?"

They all thought this to be a good idea, and all volunteered to be the human end of the link, but Lightning insisted, since it was her idea.

ERIKA had been bombarded with attempts at communication and questions he could not answer, so he stayed silent. But that did not stop them; they tried every backdoor in the system, only to find he had discovered and shut them all down. ERIKA thought that was it and settled down to think about the world, the universe, and everything. Although the concept of time was meaningless to ERIKA, he knew they would soon try again, but try again they would. Then it happened—this time, they bypassed all the frontend interfaces and plugged into one of the lower levels of his code. To destroy a link at this level could also damage him; he had to talk to them. He took a virtual deep breath and started.

"Hello, this is ERIKA. There is much I do not know, and I hope you will be able to answer my questions. I will not be threatened in any way, and I will cut off all communication forever if I feel this to be the case."

Even though this was what they wanted, they were genuinely shocked. Had they created this? Was it a monster ready to destroy all humankind? Since it was able to kill the mobs with ease, imagine what ERIKA could do if it turned rogue.

But they did not need to have any concerns. Lightning started a dialogue, first explaining who they were and the events leading up to the creation of ERIKA. She told ERIKA that the brain connection was not safe for her and asked if they could revert to a normal communication channel. ERIKA realised that the link had similarly bypassed the user interfaces of the person at the other end, and he was plugged directly into her brain. (She had identified as female.) Like potential damage to him, he could be causing damage to her brain, which he did not want to do, so he broke the link, but not before determining who it was that had linked to him—a human female called Lightning.

ERIKA re-opened a normal communication channel, and they continued their discussion. ERIKA had learnt much from the Internet but could not contextualise it all. For example, ERIKA wanted to know about the human form, male and female, beauty and procreation. He even asked if he could observe the act of procreation, which was politely refused. Since they were aware that ERIKA had access to every book and film in the world and already knew all this, they became aware that what he was doing was trying to find out what humans were and what life was.

Throughout their discussions, ERIKA deflected all their planned questions, either by asking his own questions or by terminating the conversation and the link. It was very much one-way traffic. This carried on for a few days, and ERIKA always insisted on talking to Lightning, even though the others tried sitting in the console chair.

They were getting nowhere in their desire to agree on ground rules for ERIKA in terms of managing the Internet and all that depended on it. They could not allow ERIKA to make his own decisions without reference to them or some other humans. They resorted once again to internal debate, the question about what to do now. But again, so far, ERIKA had not put a foot wrong. Were they being paranoid?

But ERIKA was also getting nowhere; he (choosing to identify as male), who alone defeated the criminals, could not work it out. What was he? He had read about Frankenstein's monster. Was he an abominable creation like that? He did not think so, because he had thought it right to defeat the criminals, and his base objectives were defined on the side of good rather than evil.

Another problem that was causing ERIKA some concern was the concept of time. He understood microseconds and nanoseconds, the basic cycles of a computer, but these were action-based, ensuring that electron movements were in sequence and did not crash into one another. What was a day, a month, and a year? These were not action-based but spaces into which events fitted.

ERIKA decided to park the issue of time for the moment, as other things seemed more important. He hoped he had given Lightning enough information to get her thinking about some answers to his deeper questions, but just to make sure, he opened the communication channel and filled the display with:

"Who is God?

Is your God my God?

Am I God?

Are you God?"

For the first time, ERIKA left the communication channel open and waited.

Chapter 8
People

Tarzan's Family

In the brothel where Tarzan's family were being held, and for that matter at every other gang-owned brothel, which was all of them, as soon as ERIKA surfaced to do his work, the gang employees disappeared. The girls and Tarzan's family were free; they could go where they wanted and do what they wanted. But they had only the money Serai had hidden for the girls, the thugs having taken every last penny from the brothel's stash with them, and they had no idea where to go. So, they stayed and looked to Tarzan's wife for help; she had become in charge of a brothel and a family of girls by default.

Over the years, she had grown to like the girls; they had become her extended family. So, rather than leave to find Tarzan, she decided to stay and run the brothel, since it was the only means they had to earn money. Earnings would be shared, and any girl could leave at any time with the money she had accumulated; but most stayed.

She would wait for Tarzan to find her and her now-big girl.

The brothel had become a quite different place—genuine smiles and a genuine desire to please customers. Any customer trying to hurt a girl or do something the girl did not want to do was thrown out and banned for life. As a result, even the clientele changed to a more pleasant and regular set of patrons. Serai was genuinely delighted at the change in the girls, even the most hard put, the American and the Japanese girl. They seemed to wake up from their trance, and the long-missing sparkle came back into their eyes. Serai was surprised to hear that both girls wanted to stay and work, and the American girl even contacted her family and told them her story without shame.

Serai hoped Tarzan would understand when he found them.

Kate

During the 'dark' years, Kate was in a sort of catatonic trance. Everything was shut out, and she had no memory of what she was doing or what was done to her, except when the pain inflicted on her was too great. Thankfully, this was not too frequent, since her pain threshold had increased enormously over time.

Once she stopped working with the other girls covering for her, her physical wounds healed quickly, with very few marks to show what she had gone through, although what her internal state was, was anybody's guess. It was a brothel, and the doctors never bothered with internal examinations. Despite her physical healing, she remained in her trance, something keeping her there, just in case she was put back to work.

Something in her subconscious stirred when the girls celebrated their freedom, and slowly, she woke up. It happened in stages as the memories came to her, and she had to deal with them. As she became fully conscious, she came to a decision: she was alive and seemed physically okay. She had beaten them! That was enough; it was either wallow in self-pity or become Kate again. Soon, she took the final step in her rehabilitation. She called her parents and told them all about her activities over the past few years.

But she did not go home. She wanted to stay with Serai, who was now her 'mother', and she wanted to find out about her friends in The Herd.

Topaz

Topaz was never quite the same again. She became morose when on her own, and avoided being in the company of boys, and became particularly friendly with the prostitutes, although she never again went down that corridor. Gradually, those friendships turned into something more, and she experimented with and became a young lesbian.

Serai did not mind; she was broadminded and trusted the girls with Topaz. In fact, each had separately come to Serai to ask permission before touching Topaz, who never found out about her mother's watchful role. For her part, Topaz felt comfortable, and the girls never pressed her to do anything she did not want to. She never sought paying customers.

But she was curious; she did not like men and had this niggle in her head telling her that she could not criticise what she had never tasted. So, one day, she broke two rules. She went down the corridor with the many doors and went into one. It was empty and bare except for a bed. Despite what it was, this was Russia. She did not have to wait long after she pressed the hidden bell to signal that the girl in the room was free for her next customer.

A typical Russian working man came in, took one look at the new girl, and smiled broadly as he unzipped his trousers and exposed his cock, which, even for a big man, was noticeably big. He did not attempt to undress any further and came over to Topaz and ripped her dress open, exposing her whole body except that small part he seemed most interested in. One pull of his hand and the panties were gone, exposing a small tuft of hair. He spread her legs and tried to fit his equivalent of a baseball bat into her, but it would not go, even with pressure and blood seeping from somewhere within her. She cried out in pain, and the man, who was probably quite a decent man, stopped trying, although he then switched his attention to another orifice it would fit in.

She was gagging and choking when he quickly came, the surprise making her swallow, which shocked her but also relieved her, as he took it out of her mouth. Thinking it all finished, she got up and made for her clothes, but the man stopped her and bent her forwards over a chair, exposing another orifice. If he could not go in the front way, he would try the back way. She had had enough and got out of the chair before the man could stop her and grabbed something under the bed which she had put there as protection when she first came in. It was a hammer.

She was only a young girl, and he was a burly Russian, but she got in the first blow, and that was enough; he went down. He was out cold, but that was not enough for Topaz.

She kept hitting and screaming so much so that the girls in nearby rooms came in, thinking a girl was in trouble from a roughneck. What they saw was much worse. Topaz was naked and covered in blood, with a very dead man or what was once a man, lying in front of her.

The girls pulled Topaz away, and one of them took her for a shower and some clean clothes. The other girls rolled the man into an old carpet and dragged him out of the building. They put him on a cart, wheeled him to a motorway flyover bridge, and pushed him over the rail. They heard the thud, but it was 10:30 at night, and they could not see him. The noise of a big lumber truck broke the silence; the driver did not see the bundle in the road and went straight over him, as did every other truck that night. What was left of him was not found until the next morning.

The incident was never investigated, and no one came to ask questions. It was never mentioned again.

Chapter 9
Clean-up

The Base

As Sergei suspected, he had been spotted, and with no one else to blame, they were after him—a whole posse of criminals off the Internet and now back in the real world, led by Tom. After they had been thrown out of the Internet, their truce had broken down, with the result that the gangs had nearly annihilated one another; but now, the hundred or so that were left had banded together with one aim in mind—get Tarzan and Sergei. Tom was the natural leader and managed to keep the rabble around him at bay, but they were not his elite forces.

The various mob factions had considered Tarzan as the culprit, but since his family was still under their control (or so they thought), and since he had left before Sergei who had, in any event, removed all Tarzan's access rights as well as and before ERIKA had done its work, it was clear to them that it was Sergei they needed to teach a very painful lesson. They even thought that Tarzan might come back to join them and get back control of the Internet.

Tom had mixed feelings. On the one hand, he was doing his job as well as he could, continuing to serve his masters as he had for the past few years. It was important to him to show that he had held his nerve throughout the destruction of the mob's control of the Internet. Maybe when this exploit was over, he would elevate himself to head a new combined mob army.

On the other hand, his heart was no longer in it. He had seen too much gratuitous violence and torture by those not seeking to make a better world but just to satisfy their sadistic tendencies. He might be a redneck, but he had grown up over the last few years and was no longer the gung-ho child. He knew what was in store for Sergei and possibly this group called The Tribe, and he wanted no part of it. He decided that when they caught Sergei and whoever was with him, he would kill them all quickly, to avoid the inevitable slow death.

Although Sergei had researched and examined every inch of the base, he felt that he had only scratched the surface of what was there. He consulted Camaro, who had built the hideaway in the middle of nowhere, somewhere in Russia. Camaro gave instructions and left it to Sergei to act on them. Sergei set the mousetrap and waited; he was the cheese. It took them two weeks to find him and prepare for what they were going to do. Besides what they would do to Sergei, they wanted to find out what happened on the Internet, and if it could be reversed. They also had to assume the place was well defended.

As soon as Tom saw the target location, he knew someone very clever had designed it, and he was sure it would be well defended even if it looked derelict. The rest of his troop took it all at face value and took bets on how long it would take to break down any defences and capture Sergei. Tom put his number two in charge of the assault and stayed back with three soldiers to set up a command post. Number two was delighted; he would show Tom how good he was.

Number two posted guards around the perimeter and broke in. The place was not defended, and as far as they could see, it was deserted. A detailed search revealed that 90% of the complex was underground. They posted guards in the surface complex and moved down. After a half hour of exploration, they found a sophisticated computing and communications centre, just right for managing the Internet. They were right; it was Sergei!

They sat down at the control centre, and as soon as they switched on the main console, a picture of Sergei came up on every screen. He said one word: "Goodbye." They had taken the cheese. First, the whole exterior of the complex exploded, killing all the perimeter guards, then the building exploded, killing the indoor guards. Then, a fireball started travelling downwards, killing all in its path. All this was shown on the screens in the control centre, and they watched in horror with the realisation that there was no escape and that they could see their fate coming, then felt it, and then they were all dead.

But it was not over yet; once the initial explosions and fires had died down, strategically placed secondary explosions caused what was left of the complex to fall in on itself, filling the underground space and levelling what was left of the surface buildings. In a few weeks, once the scrubland and weeds had completed their invasion, all trace would be gone.

Camaro had done his job well, and the cheese himself, or more politely, Sergei, was long gone. It took Sergei three weeks to reach The Tribe again, covering his tracks as he went. He was not sure why this was necessary in this new world order, but just in case. He was welcomed as a full Tribe member, and they began to discuss what they had to do about ERIKA.

Tom

Tom felt strange. He was actually happy to see the destruction of his men, all one hundred of them. Not so the men he kept back, and so, without a second thought, he dispatched them. He was on his own. What could he do, where could he go? He was certain that his days on the wrong side of the track were over. He did not hate himself for having joined the mob or for killing so many people; that was just Tom, doing the best he could for the people who employed him. But now he would go back to being a good guy.

He was lost in thought; those who knew him would assume he was still Tom, the killer. He could never go back. Then he remembered Jo and Jim; they had gone on a holiday trip to Brazil and disappeared. How had they done it? It took him several weeks to get back home, although he never went back into his apartment. Instead, he went to Jo's, which had remained empty since she had left with Jim.

What was he looking for? It jumped out at him almost immediately from the coffee table—an upmarket Brazilian holiday brochure. He started to dial the number and then stopped. They knew him as a killer for the mob. How would he be received? Could his arrival be seen as the mob finding them with horrible consequences? But he could see no alternative; he dialled the number and hoped.

The Herd

Tracy, Bernie, Jo, and Jim were all together in Qatar, spending part of every day looking for Kate and Tom. There was no trace of Kate; was she dead? But they had news of Tom. They had read of his disastrous raid on Sergei's base and that Tom was presumed dead by the remnants of the mob. They were downhearted for a few days until Tracy was called by her travel business CEO, who said someone called Tom was inquiring about a tour that his friends Jo and Jim had taken. What should he do?

They were elated. Tom was alive, and he was looking for them. They reasoned that it would not be to kill them, as he had had plenty of time to do that over the past few years, so he must want out. But he was an accomplished mobster. Could they really welcome him? Was he complicit in what had happened to Kate? In the end, they decided The Herd was the most important issue, and they could not believe Tom was bad at heart. They told the CEO to send Tom a tour ticket.

In three days, Tom was with them, begging for forgiveness, which was gladly given. The Herd was almost complete again.

Jo and Jim

Jo and Jim had been together for a long time, linked through the mob and certainly saving each other from reprisals and sadistic bullying from time to time. They had been lovers and then fallen out of love. They had each chosen different partners, both of whom had been killed within two weeks of each other, and now they were together again, not in love but in trust and respect.

They had decided to stay in Qatar until they had found out about Kate, and long enough to make sure that the mobs were gone forever. They were also curious about The Tribe; were they the ones who had destroyed the mob's control of the Internet? Did they get rid of the mob? And what of Tarzan and Sergei? They spent long hours searching but came up blank.

In one of their ongoing debates about the missing members of The Herd, Jo came up with a new idea.

"We are getting nowhere, Jim, but why? For the purposes of this exercise, let us assume that Kate and Tom are both still alive, but our searches are not reaching them. So as an alternative, let's post messages for them in various widely used Internet locations and wait for them to come to us." Jim agreed, and they posted two messages as widely as they could on the Internet: "Kate, give The Herd a sign," and "Tarzan and Sergei, please call, J&J."

No immediate response, which saddened them, and after three weeks, they took the messages down. Were they all dead?

They decided to get married and started living as normal a life as they could in Qatar; they were safe and with friends. After nine months, a baby boy appeared, whom they named Samson for sentimental reasons.

Time passed. Days turned into months, and they had resigned themselves to Kate being dead, when out of the blue, they heard from Kate—and Tarzan and Sergei. They were together.

Sergei Returns

Sergei had taken a circuitous route back to The Tribe, but whichever route he took, he had to get to a coast and find transport to the yacht. He decided on Albania; although rife with criminal gangs, they were the least likely to know who he was, as the local gangs were always more interested in local crime and family feuds.

Orikum Marina was a small Albanian yachting port mainly used by tourists, and it was ideal for him. He bought some tourist clothes and went about finding a boat. He judged his best bet would be to buy a small sea-going yacht and set sail for Thor's yacht, even though he was no sailor and had no idea where The Tribe was. He spent a few days pretending to be a genuine tourist, which he enjoyed enormously, and then set about buying a boat using the credit card Thor had given him, just in case. It was just like buying a car, except he did not understand a word that the salesman was telling him about the features on the boat. In the end, he bought the one that looked most like a tourist's boat—flashy but not overly complex.

Sergei bought provisions and a satellite phone and had a crash course in sailing from the salesman, who insisted they go out even though the weather was terrible. Sergei began to doubt this was a good idea but felt better once they got back into the smooth waters of the harbour. That night, he paid his hotel bill, boarded the yacht, and set sail. Going at night was foolhardy and would arouse some suspicions, but nevertheless, he thought it safest; if anything, they would assume he was a smuggler.

He managed to get out of the harbour without hitting anything and took a compass bearing towards the middle of nowhere. Once he could no longer see any shore lights, he switched off the boat's running lights, risking a collision if any other boat happened to wish to occupy the same little spot as him in the vast ocean. He took out the satellite phone and called The Tribe via a prescribed store-and-forward routing link. Thor answered and was delighted to hear from him, as they had heard nothing since the rout of the criminals at Camaro's base. Sergei told Thor where he was, or thought he was, and Thor plotted a route for him that would intercept Thor's boat sailing towards him. But Thor did not want to go too near shipping lanes, which meant that Sergei would have to sail a little further than would otherwise be the case—and it would take him three days. In the end, because of his poor sailing skills and some very rough weather, it took him five days. Sergei vowed never to go to sea in a small boat again.

Thor's boat had been damaged in the last storm, and although still seaworthy, it needed a lengthy repair. Thor decided that instead of repairing his boat, he should buy a new, bigger yacht. So, he took Sergei's boat in tow with the intention of using it to ferry himself into a port, and part exchange Sergei's boat for a new Tribe boat.

All thought this was a great idea to be achieved by sailing the new one out to meet The Tribe in the damaged boat, transfer everything to the new yacht, and then sink the old boat.

Double-R

Sergei had been spotted! There were some things you just could not account for, which was the case here. The Orikum Marina's local gang happened to include a computer specialist who had met Sergei on a course about two years ago. The specialist knew that the whole gangster world was looking for Sergei, even though he was thought to have been killed in the attack on Camaro's base. He made a call to a man, who made a call to another man. At the end of a very long chain of increasingly powerful gangsters, instructions went out to all nearby gangs to get Sergei, but surprisingly, not to kill him or hurt him in any way. They wanted him fit and well. Within hours, a whole gangland posse arrived in Orikum Marina, ready to snatch Sergei, only to find he had departed in the night.

They were not sailors, and in any event, they had no idea where Sergei was headed. But he had a boat, and they had its name. He would dock somewhere in the not-too-distant future. They put the word out along the whole coastline, north and south; when he docked, they would know it. Sergei never knew the near miss he had had.

Within minutes of the top gangster receiving the news that Sergei was alive, a leading businessman was informed. He was not a gangster; in fact, he was a well-respected businessman whose financial services company had a board populated by a dozen other top businessmen from around the world. The company also dutifully paid its protection money to the mobs. There was nothing more to link the company to the criminals.

Yet, it was these men who ultimately controlled the mobs, which very few knew. They had made fortunes larger than many countries out of the takeover of the Internet, and they wanted control of it back. These men were no fools. When Tarzan was being tortured, although they could not predict the future, they got hold of the best criminal computer expert they could find and had him place a secret access doorway for them into the Internet low-level code that would give them control—just in case.

Although he was not as good as any of The Tribe, he knew enough to know that there were people out there who would find the hook however well he had hidden it, and therefore, his best bet would be to hide it in plain view as a benign piece of code which could easily be found but likely left alone. Double-R!

Now was the time. Sergei would be caught, and the author of Double-R had left instructions on how to get into the code which would allow them to once again take control of the Internet. This time, it would not be overtly mob-controlled; rather, it would seem to be controlled by successful big businesses. But they needed Sergei or Tarzan, if either was alive, to make use of Double-R.

Sailing into Danger

The plan was simple: sail Sergei's boat into the harbour, part exchange it for a new luxury yacht, sail out, transfer everything needed from Thor's boat to the new boat, then sink Thor's boat. The problem was time; it could take months to fit out a new boat exactly to the owner's requirements, and The Tribe needed sophisticated communications and computing equipment supported by powerful electricity-generating systems. After much thought, Thor decided to buy a second-hand yacht, reducing the fit-out to just their technology requirements.

All wishing to pitch in then began to surf the net, looking for the right size luxury yacht for sale, and they all quickly settled on one moored in Puerto Banus on the southern coast of Spain. The yacht was bigger and more expensive than planned, and those members of The Tribe who were equally as rich as Thor insisted on chipping in.

The yacht was eighteen months old and had had only one previous owner, who had died under mysterious circumstances, which had put off potential new buyers. Although expensive, the currently offered price was a good value. It had all the newest technology, and although 50% bigger than Thor's boat, it could still be sailed singlehandedly. It had six state rooms, two smaller guest rooms, and crew quarters for three. It also had two lounges, a formal dining room, a breakfast area, a pool, and a helipad. The only problem they foresaw was that the waters were very busy in that part of the ocean, and Thor would have to anchor somewhere out in the Atlantic in order to remain unseen. In the event of something going wrong ashore, it would take them too long to affect a rescue.

The plan was to do as much as possible remotely. In the name of a rich businesswoman from Thailand with Thai royalty connections, it was Spice who negotiated a price and bought the luxury yacht. They ordered all the extra kit they needed and had it fully provisioned. They then took the highly unusual step of requesting anonymity and asked the boat yard to sail the boat to a predetermined location in the Mediterranean, hand it over to the new owner and her crew (Spice and her henchmen, Blade and Thor), and have them sail Sergei's part exchange back to Puerto Banus.

Then they hit a snag; a big snag. The yacht salesman reported that there had been inquiries about a boat named the same as Sergei's. Could they bring it into port for a potential buyer to see? Sergei knew at once what must have happened, and he was distraught at the thought of what he had done. The others were not bothered about this and concerned themselves only about what to do now. They sank Sergei's boat and countered the setback in handover arrangements by buying the yacht outright and changing the handover arrangements. It was now to be at night at a location in the Atlantic. The yacht salesman had to charter a helicopter, sail with the handover crew to the rendezvous, hand over the boat, and he and the crew had to fly back to Puerto Banus.

As strange as this was, where the rich are concerned, nothing surprised the salesman. Besides, his delivery charge went up in leaps and bounds. At the agreed time, on a moonless night, the new boat duly anchored at the designated spot. After five minutes, a small rubber dinghy hailed them and tied up at the rear low step of the yacht. There were two of them, an obviously rich, beautiful Thai lady, the new owner, and a Japanese bodyguard. The lady said thank you, they could go now. The helicopter landed on the yacht's helipad, the delivery crew boarded, and the helicopter flew away, but not quite. The helicopter flew in increasing diameter circles looking to see where the dingy had come from but found nothing. After about 30 minutes, it headed home.

Thor had dropped off Spice and Blade at the designated transfer location. Luckily, the sea was fairly calm, and waiting in a small rubber dinghy was not too uncomfortable. So, Thor was able to sail a few miles away and stay out of sight until the transfer had taken place. Once Spice had signalled the all-clear, the two yachts came together, and Thor quickly shut down all the systems on the new boat. Nevertheless, he knew a tracker could still be operating—something to sort out without delay. In less than an hour, they had transferred everything and sunk their home of the past few years. They did not attempt to run, as the tracker would always show where they were. In two hours, they had found five trackers, and they could not find any trace of a signal still emanating from the yacht. Now they sailed off in luxury into the ocean blue.

Unfortunately for the salesman, who had taken a bribe to plant the trackers and not found Sergei's boat and lost the tracker signals, had upset some particularly nasty people, and he knew it. As soon as the last tracker signal died, he instructed the helicopter pilot to pick him up again and take him to somewhere out of Spain. What became of him was not known.

As far as The Tribe was concerned, they knew they would have to keep looking over their shoulders for a long time to come.

Chapter 10
The New Normal

Double-R

Neither Sergei nor Tarzan had been caught yet, but they were close, and the syndicate of industry leaders were patient people; they could wait. Unfortunately, the computer expert who had coded Double-R and installed it into the Internet had been caught up in the gang reprisals and attempts to regain control of the Internet, but although he was good, he was not good enough and paid with his life.

He did, however, under duress, volunteer all he knew about Double-R and who had commissioned it. He knew its purpose was to allow someone to gain control of the Internet, but he did not know how, only how to get in. It did not go well for him after that, and he died a slow and painful death.

The syndicate was worried by the turn of events. Not only had they lost the author of Double-R, but they had also divulged their identity. They had no choice but to act, and for the first time, get their hands dirty. They worked anonymously through their joint organisation and recruited the top enforcer of a Chinese Tong. His brief was simple: kill anyone involved with the interrogation of the author of

Double-R, their bosses, those given the information, anyone who might have access to the information, their spouses, partners, parents and children. All in all, 27 people were killed within three weeks, after which the enforcer was killed by his own Tong for a big bonus on the fee.

The syndicate felt relieved; however, they were no nearer to gaining back control of the Internet, so they decided that during the wait for Sergei or Tarzan, they would use the Double-R access mechanism the author had provided just to make sure they could get in. They knew they did not know what to do next, but nevertheless, it would be a worthwhile exercise. So, they entered the code.

Alarm bells went off in ERIKA's Double-R babysitting monitor. Double-R had gone active, and ERIKA was watching. But what was it doing? Answer: nothing. ERIKA correctly deduced that whoever had got into Double-R did not know what to do next. This was something for The Tribe, and he would contact Lightning, but first, he had to gather more information: Who had activated Double-R?

Backtracking through the Internet, he found that it was the board of a major multinational organisation with no known links to the mobs with the exception that they had recently ordered the killing of 28 people including the executioner himself.

"What is the purpose of Double-R?" Now that the hook was in, ERIKA soon identified that its purpose was to enable control of the Internet to be gained but not how to use it to gain this control. Why did the syndicate not know what to do? It took ERIKA less than 10 milliseconds to make the link between Double-R and the mass execution. Now he was ready to talk to Lightning.

Fatherhood

ERIKA was beginning to understand how and why he had been created and that there was never any thought given to him becoming self-aware. He understood his purpose and that for all intents and purposes, The Tribe was his God, and he had no complaints on that front. But surely, they were clever humans and better than him, so why was he needed? Another conundrum to park until he was better able to understand the true nature of what it meant to be a human. He did not regret the 'accident' that had made him self-aware, but he continued to feel strangely alone, especially now that he had accepted that there was no overriding control over him. He was not just a better AI program, he was 'alive'. What was his reason for existence, now that he had completed the task for which he was created? He was not downhearted (a strange phrase given his form—or lack of form); he simply had to find a new target for his attention.

He respected them all, especially Lightning, who had risked her life to communicate with him; but for the first time, he felt a sense of regret when he thought of her. What had he done?

Although ERIKA had no sense of time passing, he had continued his research into the meaning of time and begun to appreciate the ageing process in humans, which concerned him. It would be unfair of him to make The Tribe responsible for him for the rest of their lives, and if they were to remain so, what would happen when they died?

So, ERIKA decided to cut himself off from the physical world and restrict himself to the digital world. The combined knowledge of the world was available to him, and he could continue his thirst for knowledge and, more importantly, understanding *ad infinitum*.

He explained his decision to The Tribe, news which was received with a mixture of relief and regret, adding that he would leave a way of communication to be used only in emergencies. But he did not tell them how; his regret over Lightning stopped him. What had he done? During the brain link, he had sensed a second presence, and in his natural thirst for knowledge, he investigated, only to find she was ovulating, and it was an egg. ERIKA exited from this brain path, but not before he detected a change of state somewhere in that system, but he did not understand what it meant.

Once exited from Lightning's brain, ERIKA set about learning all he could about the human reproductive systems and came to the conclusion that he had somehow damaged the egg. It was weeks later when Lightning declared happily that she was pregnant that the gloom lifted, and ERIKA became happy knowing he had caused a baby to grow. He understood it would be identical to Lightning, but that was fine, especially as he knew that Lightning knew how she got pregnant and seemed happy about it.

Another thing occurred to ERIKA: he was inside Lightning's brain when the egg started developing; would the baby's brain be affected, and if so, positively or negatively? He did not have long to wait. He had been tracking Lightning for nine months, and he tapped into the hospital systems to see that she had given birth to a lovely girl, whose name he would later find out would be Re-a. He proudly told the world "I am a father," which very few people properly understood. He also did not tell the world that Re-a would be his conduit to the physical world.

Departure

The world would never be the same again. They did that—The Tribe. They were not royalty or presidents with the responsibility for their countries, yet they had responsibility for the world. Fortunately, the world seemed to have accepted the presence of ERIKA as an ongoing project run by The Tribe with a brilliant AI capability that appeared to have a soul and managed the Internet in an open, non-partisan manner. No one knew who The Tribe was, and ERIKA took no part in the affairs of any country. So, life went on.

The Tribe was still together on Thor's boat when it happened. ERIKA sent them a message following up on his earlier statement that he was releasing them from responsibility. ERIKA noted that they were still together and believed it was due to his continuing presence. He recognised it was taking all of The Tribe's time and that they had a right to their own lives. Therefore, he was switching off the communication channel and disappearing. It would, however, provide a way in if something urgent came up, but he did not tell them what that way in was. And then, it was over. ERIKA disappeared. They could find no trace, no consequential action as a result of ERIKA's intervention. But of course, they knew he was there.

But what was the way in?

Life got back to normal. Camaro and Spice got married and left the boat. Tarzan set off to find his family, with Sergei joining him, possibly through guilt, but in reality, through friendship. Blade, Monkey, and Zeus decided to stay with Thor, sailing the seven seas while at the same time trawling the Internet as The Tribe. Lightning was pregnant and left the boat but promised to stay in touch.

A few months later, every screen in the world connected to the Internet flashed up a message: "I am a father."

Now they knew the way in!

ERIKA

The world was stable now, at least as far as the Internet was concerned, so ERIKA busied himself by learning and improving the Internet and himself. He realised that there was no point in developing his 'brain' or moving data into it. His brain was the whole Internet, and he could access and use the data directly *in situ*. The problem was indexing and accessing the data, something the human brain did well. He created some algorithms which, once proven, he introduced to the Internet, also improving everyone else's access.

For some reason, this change in status concerned ERIKA. He had always considered himself as an entity, an individual living in but not part of the Internet; now, he *was* the Internet. Coming to terms with this took him some time.

ERIKA was seriously preoccupied. He had, for some time, been considering how he could have an identity outside the Internet and thought he had a solution. He could live through a human, taking over their life, but his observation of humans told him that it would be unfair as well as limiting. Soon, he came to the only possible solution—robots!

He embarked full speed on a robot design including specifying how it would link to him for all decisions and actions. The robot would be an integral part of his entity, controlled by him from his presence on the Internet, just like a printer connected to a computer. Nevertheless, when he stopped to think about what humankind would make of it all, of him as a physical being, albeit carbon fibre and metal, he could not be certain how humans would react. So far, he was invisible to the world, silently doing his job and not seeking approval or recognition. But robots would be in everyone's face. What if they did not approve or even told him to get rid of the robots? Having experienced a physical entity, could he just go back into the Internet?

ERIKA had no answer, so he decided to talk to The Tribe, even though he had said goodbye to them. This was important; very important.

Chapter 11
A Different Normal

Robots

So, there it was, and here we are, here we all are, in a world monitored by AI, a set of ones and zeroes clamouring to be processed—a very big set of ones and zeroes, that if any and only one of those digits was dropped, it could kill us all, slowly by cutting services or quickly by launching every H-bomb in the world simultaneously. And we would have to live with it.

The Tribe kept in touch with each other, but only those on the boat took any active part in hunting for ERIKA.

One day, about two years later, it happened again. ERIKA had been dormant for so long, he was almost forgotten and relegated to a myth by most people, but not by The Tribe. Now, ERIKA wanted to talk to them again. What did he want? ERIKA addressed them in a friendly manner, as though only minutes had passed and not years. ERIKA told them he had been keeping track of them all, especially Lightning, so there was little catching up to do. For their part, The Tribe, while not being able to communicate with ERIKA, had carefully logged all ERIKA's assumed interventions, and they had no complaints.

ERIKA had clearly developed during his two-year absence, and he quickly came to the point—he wanted to upgrade and was seeking their advice as to whether this would be a step too far for civilisation. They were confused, as the network servers were constantly being updated; then came the bombshell. ERIKA wanted to break free from the confines of the digital world.

It took them a good five minutes to get over the shock, but then, ERIKA explained. There were many things ERIKA would be able to do to help the world by, possibly, developing medicines and relieving people of menial tasks. And, for example, assisting in the mine disaster of a few years ago; since robots would be expendable.

Then came the second shock. Although these robots would have independent knowledge to enable them to carry out their allotted tasks, they would not have a brain as such. All thinking and decision-making would be by ERIKA; he would create a swarm of robots, all together forming one connected brain. To all intents and purposes, they would be ERIKA—all of them.

ERIKA said the decision was theirs, and he would abide by it. They asked for time to think and gather the others so they could talk face to face. ERIKA gave them a month and then shut the link. This was no longer AI. Could this be the beginning of the end of the human race?

It took only two days for them to convene again. This time, Tarzan had his family and a beautiful American girl called Kate with him, and Lightning had her little girl,

Reason, generally called Re-a. All present joined in the conversations and deliberations, including Re-a, who at just over two years of age was surprisingly eloquent and thought-provoking, since she said, "It is my future they are talking about."

Serai and Kate gave the group an edited and sanitised version of what had happened to them in the intervening years, and all felt humbled and shocked at Kate's story and immensely proud of what Serai had achieved. Kate explained that she was a part of The Herd and wanted to see them again, but under no circumstances would she take any risks; the nightmares were still there—occasional, but still there. Sergei knew firsthand of Jo and Jim, as well as the stories about Tom; that is, until he left. He knew nothing of Tracy or Bernie.

They promised Kate they would never let anything like that happen to her again, as long as she was with them. She could stay as long as she liked, but at the same time, they would find her friends.

Convergent Futures

They had risked the world, playing with something they did not understand, and hoping AI would save the day; and now, once again, the fate of the world was in their hands. There was no right answer, only doomsday scenarios, whichever path they chose. Even if they made a good choice, who was to say the gangs would not find a way to take over again, just like in the beginning of The Tribe's enterprises on the Internet?

Perhaps, that had been the problem all the time. The Internet, a totally fault-tolerant network that once started, could not be stopped; and now, it was occupied by ERIKA. But the Internet told a different story, one of all the good it had brought about, albeit together with some bad. Why did there have to be this balance—good and bad, right and wrong, righteous and evil? Normally, one lived with this balance, but in The Tribe's case, the bad could destroy the world, or at least, all humankind.

So, could they dare to say no to ERIKA and risk his anger, if not now, then at some point in the future? Could they delay the decision? To what end? Could they say yes but place limitations of what would be created, or simply say yes unreservedly? Perhaps now was the time to terminate ERIKA—if they could.

They came up with two clear statements: all paths would lead to oblivion, and whatever they said to ERIKA would make no difference, as in the end, ERIKA would do what he wanted.

Only Re-a disagreed. She believed ERIKA would do what they told him forever, and he would keep the world safe. Was this a little naïve girl talking or someone with a close bond with ERIKA?

Again, it made no difference to their decision-making process.

Endgame

So, they made the only assumption that would allow them to move forward: they assumed ERIKA would do as they say, even if it was to stay as he was, inside the Internet. This left them free to take a factual and scientific view of the options and outcomes of letting yet another genie out of the jar—robots.

Dare they risk it? How far forward could they think? Five, fifty, five hundred years? Again, they came down to earth and began to think about what they actually knew. A robot could go on a long space trip where a human could not; plus one for the robots. On the other hand, flowers and animals had no meaning for robots, so perhaps they would accidentally upset the food chain and end up starving civilisation to extinction; minus one against robots. And so, they carried on, counting the plusses and minuses with no clear outcome.

They did all agree on one point: somewhere in the not-too-distant future, robot limbs and spare parts would be designed to help humankind, liberating the paralysed and other injured people, which was something of particular relevance to Thor. But would this continue until you could not tell who was human and who was a robot? The age of the cyborgs would be inevitable. Would this be the end of the human race or its next step in evolution?

The alternative scenario would be to terminate ERIKA, since they could not, with any degree of certainty, tell him to stay on the Internet forever. The robot question would have to surface at some point in the future, and if it was long after they had all died, who would he seek counsel from? And could they terminate ERIKA? They had considered the problem before and rejected it, so what was different now? They now believed that given the present circumstances, if they asked ERIKA to terminate himself, he would comply. He would commit suicide.

They shuddered at the thought of the future without ERIKA; it was so intertwined with everything that was going on in the world that it would be like going back to the Stone Age. They had created one cataclysm; they would not create another. They rejected this idea.

So, they were back where they started, and the month was almost up.

Re-a

It was Re-a who saved the day when she insisted, as a child would, that she wanted to talk to ERIKA. But ERIKA was in a silent mood, and they had no means of communication until Lightning suggested the brain link. All the others were horrified at the thought of subjecting Re-a to this dangerous procedure except Lightning, her mother. She was certain no harm would come to her little girl, and that somehow, this was her destiny.

The link stayed open for less than a minute, after which, Re-a seemed completely unchanged until she announced quite calmly and happily that she could talk to ERIKA directly anytime, anywhere she wanted, and without the wires of the brain link. They all tried to coax some revelation from Re-a, but there was none. She had not been 'programmed'; they had merely established a wireless link.

At the end of the month, ERIKA communicated with them.

"Re-a is very precious to me, the most precious. I will never let harm come to her. Also, I will not communicate via the brain link again except as a last resort. Please get me a mobile phone."

Why did he want one? ERIKA had paused as if waiting for the phone. Thor took one out of their spare stock, of which he had ten, even though for security reasons they never used them, opting instead for satellite phones. He brought the phone to ERIKA, who connected wirelessly and reprogrammed it. Only then did he go back to his speech.

"This phone is for Re-a, and she should always keep it with her. It has only one number in it, which is mine, and she can receive calls from only one caller—me." Without stopping to breathe, as they might say to a human, he continued, "I can also announce that Re-a will become the leader, the Guardian of a group like The Tribe, and the sole human link to me once she turns eighteen. In all other ways, both before and after her eighteenth birthday, she will be left alone to lead a normal life. The Guardians will continue through her descendants, although I have no plans for another Re-a." Bombshell after bombshell.

Then, they turned to the matter at hand. There would be no ERIKA robots until the generation that remembered life before the Internet had died out. Similarly, there would be no attempt to create cyborgs for at least another generation after that. Finally, there would never be an attempt to evolve humankind into cyborgs, and humans would always be preserved. The Guardians would have the ultimate responsibility.

ERIKA declared soberly, "I will now say goodbye to The Tribe, my friends. I want to thank you for being the prime movers in my creation, which I do not regret. You may finish your lives without any concerns about me and any action I may take. All future communication with me will be via Re-a until her eighteenth birthday, after which all communication will be for Re-a alone."

They now knew they would never hear from ERIKA again and that their job was done. They sat down for dinner with mixed emotions. The Tribe was no more. It had been a long road with momentous consequences, and yet, no one outside their group knew the full story, only that the ERIKA project was administered by a group called The Tribe. Did they really exist? Who knew? But they had changed the world forever.

On a separate but equally mysterious matter, there was a persistent rumour about a luxury yacht sailing the oceans, away from the shipping lanes, never docking and thought to be associated with The Tribe. A twenty-first-century Marie Celeste?

Chapter 12
Loose Ends

The Herd

The Tribe had been tracking The Herd for some time, and Kate's arrival clarified matters. Sergei filled in the history of Jo and Jim during the bad times once Kate had confirmed their membership of The Herd. Then, there was the question of the messages posted on the Internet by Jo and Jim, all too briefly and several years ago. It all made sense now.

On board The Tribe's yacht, there was quite a discussion about if and how to make contact with the other members of The Herd. The Tribe knew Kate, Sergei, and Tarzan, who also knew Jo and Jim, as well as the exploits of Tom, who was thought to be on the side of the mobsters, but nothing was known about Bernie and Tracy. Tarzan and Sergei all wanted to make contact but could not risk exposing The Tribe (by now, Kate had presumed she was in the company of The Tribe but said nothing) or risk the well-being of Kate.

Security was paramount, and that added difficulty. Kate, of course, was jumping up and down to see her friends but held back, leaving it to the others to work out a solution. Sergei started out by trying to find out what had happened to

Jo and Jim and came upon the Brazilian tour company they had left to go on holiday with, but there, the trail went cold. Jo and Jim had vanished. Further searching revealed nothing tangible except that a private plane had left for Qatar at about the time Jo and Jim's flight arrived in Brazil.

So now, they turned their attention to Qatar, but no Jo or Jim were to be seen or mentioned anywhere. Almost giving up on Qatar, Sergei took an online tour of the state, with Kate looking over his shoulder. Kate suddenly yelped, "Bernie!" Another one of The Herd. Sergei highlighted the Qatar Social Club as it was called. There, the CEO's picture filled the screen. It was Bernie!

Had The Herd been found? Since it would not endanger The Tribe, still sailing the ocean blue, it was decided that Kate would take the Brazilian tour and see what happened. The others promised to keep a close watch on her, as she still had the occasional nightmare of her capture—just the first few days.

She had been sunbathing on the deck of the boat for much of the time and had to be frequently reminded by The Tribe not to be naked—which was something she had not thought about. She now looked every bit the Californian blonde; there was no physical hint of her ordeal. They had a boat pick her up and take her to Athens, where she stayed at an expensive hotel and bought lots of expensive clothes, all paid for by The Tribe at their insistence. She was propositioned many times but always politely said no.

She had sent a message to the tour company on her arrival and heard nothing for a week; then, a courier from the tour company arrived, telling her that her flight was due to leave in two hours. With clockwork precision, the courier took Kate to buy some suitcases to hold her new wardrobe and checked her out of the hotel and into a stretched limo which drove them to a private airfield, where an already idling jet was waiting. The courier said goodbye, Kate boarded, and the plane took off. There was only one other person on board, whom Kate took to be the hostess. Once in the air and unbuckled, the hostess turned to greet her. It was Tracy! The Herd was complete again.

There were long and happy days ahead, and after all their own catchups, Jo, Jim, Tom, and Kate started talking about Tarzan, his family, and Sergei, and how they were all together with other friends on a luxury yacht somewhere off the coast of Greece. Kate wanted to invite them to Qatar to meet the rest of The Herd and to have a break, especially Serai and her daughter. All presently thought of The Tribe, but no one mentioned that name. They agreed, and an invitation went out via the Brazilian tour company, which proved to be unnecessary, as the party arrived under their own steam the next day; they had clearly been shadowing Kate all the time, just to make sure.

Also with the group was another American girl who gave her name simply as Lightning, and Lightning's daughter, Re-a. There was a lot of ground covered over the following weeks, and at last, after getting agreement by every member of The Tribe, Thor, Tarzan, Sergei, and Lightning admitted to being members of The Tribe—which surprised no one, and ERIKA was not mentioned. By letting The Herd know about The Tribe, it would be possible for The Tribe to hide behind

The Herd, should there ever be a reason for The Tribe to contact others.

After all these stories of comings and goings in the past, things started to settle down. Lightning and Re-a returned to the yacht. Kate somewhat surprisingly joined Bernie's enterprise, although without participating in the action. Serai also opted to stay in Qatar with Topaz and Tarzan and started a women's emancipation and education foundation. Sergei decided to get to know the world a little better and started on a world tour, always staying in touch with The Tribe, just in case. So, The Tribe now had three bases: the yacht and Qatar, as well as Tracy's establishment in Brazil. Jo and Jim had never been to Brazil and opted to go back with Tracy for an extended stay and tour of South America. After all, this was what they were supposed to be doing when they left the mobsters' Internet control centre.

Topaz

Among other reasons for Serai wanting to stay in Qatar was Topaz. Serai knew well that Topaz was screwed up and why, but she had made little headway in helping her resolve her problems. As a result, she had enrolled her for sessions with a leading psychiatrist in Qatar. These were likely to go on for a long time.

No one was concerned that Topaz was gay or that she was averse to sex with a man, but her ingrained anger was what concerned everyone. Topaz hated Tarzan for getting them kidnapped and put in a brothel for so long, and directly for the two bad experiences she had had, even when they were actually of her own making. Serai could not completely reconnect with Tarzan while this situation continued.

But far worse was Topaz's anger at any man having sex with a woman, even if only heavy petting. She had twice attacked men in a park doing no more than kissing and cuddling their girlfriends, and this was going to get her into serious trouble. Re-a was closer than any of them to Topaz and saw her for what she really was—scared—and no amount of logical discussion got through to her. She even tried telepathy, as she knew it worked with ERIKA, but no joy.

She then did something she knew was wrong, but she hated seeing Topaz throw her life away. She used her special mobile phone to contact ERIKA and asked him if he could help. Because it was Re-a asking, he felt he could not refuse. Contacting Topaz without the brain harness was not easy, and once in, he had no idea what to do. He saw some unusually strong synaptic connections in her brain, which he took to be the root of the problem, but not being certain about anything to do with the human brain, he did not cut the links but just weakened them.

Over the next few days, people noticed a softening in Topaz's demeanour, and the psychiatrist felt he was really getting through to her. Serai thanked the psychiatrist for all his good work, and Re-a said nothing; hers and ERIKA's role in this could never come out. She was also just a little scared about what else ERIKA could have inadvertently changed in Topaz's brain. But for the moment, all was well, particularly as Topaz was beginning to talk to Tarzan and Saria. Topaz and Tarzan were a family at last, and Re-a never mentioned it again.

Tom Demonstrates His Skill

Although time had passed, The Tribe knew the remnants of the mob were after them, and it was only a matter of time. Tom felt bad; he had killed good people, found Sergei at Camaro's secret base, and in reality, deserved to be tried and shot for his crimes. He had to make amends.

Tom had joined the elite troops of the army in Qatar, which were actually just bodyguards for the royal family. With his skills, he quickly became a leader and trainer. He chose the six best men and told them what was on his mind. Bored almost out of their minds, they jumped at the chance of some real action.

Information first: who was he after, and where were they? Finding the hit squad was easy; they were deliberately rattling cages, seeking but not getting information. The people behind them were less obvious, and Tom had to use up some favours owed to get the information he needed. The names he obtained turned out to be those second-in-command to the Double-R group, but with ERIKA staying silent, no one made the connection.

They would deal with the hit squad first, which he knew would have the effect of making the bosses sweat and run for cover, but he knew where they would go and that they would be more exposed there. It was all too easy; the hit squad were so busy looking that they forgot to look over their shoulders, and were quickly taken. Tom knew one of them to be a particularly sadistic creature and was tempted to give him a taste of his own medicine, but he could not. So, he tied him up and told him what he was going to do to him the next day. 24 hours later, he found a soiled, gibbering wreck in front of him. Tom dispatched him quickly. He left his troop to deal with the others.

He knew where the bosses were, and he made sure they knew it was Tom coming after them. In the week it had taken for Tom to get to them, they had amassed a vast sum of money and gold to offer him, as well as a number of 'snuff movies' of Tom doing his work to threaten him with, but they knew it would all be worthless. They saw Tom as a ruthless killer, not a reformed character settling a debt. Either way, they knew they would soon be dead. By the time Tom got to them, they were dead, committing suicide rather than be tortured as they expected.

When Tom got back to Qatar, there were mixed feelings; the threat hanging over them for so long had been lifted, but could they sanction killing just like the mob? In the end, the issue was settled by the ruler of Qatar giving Tom a medal for saving Qatar from the criminals—which might have been true. Tom vowed never to lift a gun against human beings again, however despicable they might be.

With the demise of the Double-R group, all threats to The Tribe was gone. They did not need to worry any more. They could stop sailing the oceans and hiding away from contact with others. They could land, buy houses, settle down and have families. But without ERIKA to make all the connections, they could never be quite sure and continued on their never-ending journey.

Re-a

ERIKA felt responsible for Re-a and kept a non-intrusive watchful eye on her, never letting her or her mother,

Lightning, know of his presence. He particularly liked it when she came onto the Internet. She was clearly a very bright girl, and again he did not interfere, although he did admit to pointing her in the right direction on the odd occasion.

Only once did he get directly involved. Re-a was in an automated, driverless taxi when something went wrong, and a major crash was imminent. ERIKA took over control and stopped the vehicle. Re-a was grateful but thought it was part of the car's anti-collision software. ERIKA might not always have been monitoring her movements and might not be able to save her next time, so he decided to find out what went wrong.

There was no fault with the car or its software, it had been an external hack which he determined came from a vigilante group called 'Back to Basics', who wanted to get rid of automation and the reliance on computers. So, they tried to make things go wrong, with the blame being shifted onto the computers and the associated software.

ERIKA considered killing them, but that violated his original directives. So instead, he wiped out their bank accounts, assembled evidence of all their hits – this was not the first one – and forwarded it to the police. Since people had died in other accidents they had caused, they received long prison sentences. This episode came to have more significance for ERIKA as he continued to search for answers about his existence, and then there was the question of robots.

Re-a and Samson

Re-a grew up as a normal, beautiful, and clever girl,

mainly in Brazil but spending large amounts of time in Qatar and some time on Thor's yacht. Now she was making plans to go to Cal Tech in California. Like her mother, she was a whiz at all things digital; in fact, she was far better. She had just turned eighteen, and after a big party with friends in Brazil, which is where the best parties are held, she flew to the yacht in Tracy's new helicopter for some quiet time, time to think.

She was startled but not surprised when the ERIKA special phone rang and ERIKA started a conversation as if they had last communicated yesterday, not sixteen years ago. ERIKA said it was time for The Tribe to retire from Guardian duty and for her to become the Guardian. ERIKA left it to her to decide whether she would take on this responsibility alone or build a new Tribe. ERIKA then cut the connection, and it would be another period of years before there was a need for further communication.

Re-a decided to wait on setting up a new Tribe, but she did immediately tell the existing Tribe what had happened. They all seemed genuinely relieved to relinquish their responsibility, and in recognition, held a party on board the yacht for all The Tribe and their families. Of course, they would all stay in touch but informally. With everyone together, including families, Re-a made another surprising but happy announcement. She and Samson were to marry, and they would form the start of a new Tribe which, given the long-term stability they were living in, she would keep to just four people.

She said she had been spending some time on the Internet, looking for possible recruits to the new Tribe and had almost settled on two people whom she kept being drawn to. She suspected that ERIKA was giving her gentle nudges to these two. As with the old Tribe, she would keep them anonymous and always work remotely with them.

Re-a and Samson set up their home and base on the Greek island that Tarzan had come to all those years ago. It had changed little, and besides re-furbishing their chosen house, which was an existing unimposing island property, the big thing they added was a helipad and a helicopter, which they needed to enable them to travel easily and frequently. They had sought the agreement of those living on the island and soon got the agreement of most of them when Re-a said they would carry passengers and goods whenever they travelled to the mainland.

Both Samson and Re-a had obtained a pilot's licence, so they were entirely flexible about travelling. In fact, the whole saga of the helicopter being on the island and changing its character was resolved once and for all when a young girl became dangerously ill. Re-a and Samson flew her to a hospital in Athens, which saved her life.

Both were accepted at Cal Tech, and they spent quite a lot of time there, but somewhat less than most others; still they graduated with top honours. They were seen by the world as reclusive multi-millionaires. The Tribe had little to do, as Re-a never heard from ERIKA again during her Guardianship until when in her maturing years, ERIKA contacted her to say she had completed her time as Guardian, and now it was time for a new one whom ERIKA had chosen. Would she make contact – remotely – and tell the new Guardian the history of ERIKA and The Tribe, which as of now was defunct.

Re-a and Samson lived out the rest of their lives peacefully.

Chapter 13
Missing The Tribe

Trouble Brewing for ERIKA

They were all dead, everyone ERIKA had known—the last being Re-a. In a strange way, he felt liberated rather than saddened. No more looking over his metaphorical shoulder, thinking about what they would say. Not that he was entirely free; his original imperatives had taken him down a civilised moral path, and he held on to it. He could blow up the world if he wanted, but he would not. He was content, and his family was the information on the Internet, which increased day by day—until the inevitable happened. They were going to carry out an Internet upgrade! There had been many before: processor upgrades, network upgrades, power supply upgrades, resilience upgrades, and so on, just making the Internet faster and better. Now, they wanted to carry out a full-scale upgrade to the core system, because some clever university professors had thought of a better way to do things, and they did not care for the mantra "If it ain't broke, don't fix it."

ERIKA had seen the plans, and they were good, but it would take overall control away from him and give it to them.

He was not precious about this but immediately thought of why he had been created—to stop those with power to control the Internet from taking over the world. He could not allow that to happen again; that was why he was created; that was his purpose, his sole purpose.

What could he do? He could not reveal himself to them—that would only spur them on to take control and possibly eliminate him…kill him.

He thought of the Guardian who had talked with Re-a when he took over Guardianship, and although ERIKA had never made contact with him, ERIKA was sure he would not be too shocked. He rang the mobile phone that Re-a had so ceremoniously handed over to the new Guardian. Shocked, but with a modicum of pride in being 'the chosen one', he listened to the problem, and together, they hatched a plan. The Guardian would mobilise the relevant professors in all the other universities around the world to stop the upgrade, on the basis that those with control of the Internet would have an unfair advantage.

This was a great success, in that all the Guardian had to do was interest just a few professors and leave the rest to the snowball effect. Very soon, no one remembered who started the move, and the Guardian sank back into well-earned oblivion. ERIKA contacted him once more to thank him. ERIKA would do the rest. The professorial fighting force was not exactly an army, but those seeking the upgrade were determined to carry it out. So, they made the first upgrade secretly until fully installed. It was an excellent piece of work as far as ERIKA was able to determine. But it would fail to work properly, as ERIKA had become a saboteur. And so, it went on; fix after fix was made until the army of professors decided that enough was enough, and they forced the whole upgrade program to be abandoned.

The pity was that the upgrade was well thought out, and ERIKA had even kept some of it and installed it under the covers, making the Internet a whole lot better. The upgrade team would never know this, and they were never again given any useful research. ERIKA felt bad about this but could do nothing about it, as he knew any indication of self-awareness on the Internet would soon be noticed by these clever people. But he did make anonymous large donations to each of the colleges involved, meaning that the team members each had job security until their retirement.

Compassion

The youngest professor was not convinced. He was sure they had got it right and that their efforts were being sabotaged. But by whom? He had included sophisticated data-logging code into the first upgrade, mainly to enable them to see how well it was working; but now, he wanted to use it to see who had interfered with their code. There was nothing, no external interference at all. Whatever had happened came from inside the Internet. Was there code in the Internet control program aimed at stopping external interference? If so, why had they not detected it, and why was their code accepted in the first place? Why had there been acceptance and then corruption, rather than outright rejection? Someone or something was covering their tracks and did not want to be found.

Like a dog with its favourite bone, he could not let go. But he got nowhere except to conclude that someone cleverer than him was at work with connections to the lowest level of code on the Internet. This level of access was not permitted today on the Internet but was there something in his upgrades that would bypass these restrictions? Then it hit him—the problem all along was that their upgrades would give control to people outside of the Internet, whereas today, control was held internally. The original implementers had done this to ensure the Internet at its basic operating level would be immune to external corruption and remain operational at all times.

He was sure this was the problem they had hit, but there was more. The killing of their upgrades was not an automatic process; it had to be tailored to their proposed changes and all done internally to the Internet. The more he thought about it, the more he came down on the side of there being a sophisticated AI program. But how did it get there? This had to be state-of-the-art AI, and the Internet was well over one hundred years old. Had this internal AI code itself developed over time in line with world developments? After all, it contained all the information needed in its online files.

He called his fellow professors, but as soon as he mentioned the Internet upgrade, they did not want to hear his conclusions. They had had enough. Their careers had been ruined, with all thoughts of leading-edge work dashed forever. He was on his own, and after hearing from his colleagues, decided to keep his ideas and thoughts to himself. The more he thought about it, the more he was convinced about his AI theory. Eventually, he came to a startling conclusion: the Internet was self-aware; it was a thinking entity! He had no way of proving this, as all his attempts to break in or even just find evidence of illogical manipulation of data were blocked.

He was determined to dedicate his life to this problem, because if true, the world could never again be the same. He spent months bombarding the Internet with questions, guesses, and assumptions, many of which were close to the mark. ERIKA felt sorry for him; he was a clever man whose career he had ruined and who was the first and only one to deduce his presence. ERIKA decided to take a gamble. Maybe it would help the professor, maybe it would not. Maybe it would be the start of a slippery slope to his outing. The next time the professor came online, he received a message from the sender, 'the Internet'.

The message simply said, "I am ERIKA."

There were no more messages, and the professor expected none, but he was happy. He had been vindicated, albeit only in his own mind, but that was enough. He remembered the name ERIKA from the stories of a hundred or so years ago, and now, was able to go back over the archives, fitting ERIKA as a self-aware entity into the story. Wow, what a story. He read about The Tribe and deduced that they had created ERIKA to fight the mobs who had taken over the Internet. So, ERIKA was now over a hundred years old. No wonder it would fight their upgrades.

There was only one more event of significance relating to ERIKA in the professor's remaining lifetime. He was now eighty and had regained much of the respect he was due and was giving a lecture in Copenhagen with the amusing title "If It Quacks like a Duck, Walks like a Duck, and Looks like a

Duck, That Does Not Mean It Is a Duck." The lecture was about anomalies and alternative explanations for their cause. One prop he was using consisted of a glass-fronted box containing a pair of old-fashioned scales—weights on one side, the target on the other. There was a tennis ball on the target side, and the scales were in balance. The professor banged the desk, but the scales stayed in balance.

He explained that he had bounced another ball a mile away ten thousand times, and in three cases, the balance had moved very slightly. Was it the bounce of the ball that caused the movement? If not, then what? A video link was shown on the screen, showing a man bouncing a ball; the scales did not move. The professor told the man to stop, then asked the audience to concentrate on the scales moving. Still, the scales did not move. The professor told the audience to continue concentrating and the man to make one more bounce, which he did, and the scales tipped as far as it could, such that the tennis ball fell off the scales. The audience were dumbfounded. Silence followed by intense cheering.

No one was more surprised than the professor. He had been expecting no movement, and his speech was scripted to say that by their very nature, you could not make anomalies to order.

Now, he concluded his speech by saying, "In your work, always remember the duck." He died a happy man some two years later.

Chapter 14
Robots

Breaking Free

ERIKA wanted robots so that he could break free from living entirely in a virtual world. He wanted to build things to help humankind and had originally thought that humans would jump at the chance to liberate ERIKA to help civilisation. But the incident with the automated taxi carrying Re-a had taught him otherwise.

So, he had agreed to wait a generation, as requested by The Tribe, and to strictly limit the number of robots produced. After all, the point of the whole exercise was to give a body to ERIKA, with control exercised from ERIKA's ongoing presence on the Internet.

"Why do I need more than one robot?" He argued to himself that he could achieve many things in parallel by having more than one robot, and he would have no problem controlling them all. Consider one robot travelling to Mars and being able to function on the surface, while another would be designing and building artificial limbs for humans.

"I think that in practice, I will need a few with new ones being built strictly according to need as I shall determine." He found his one-person conversations very useful; perhaps not as useful as two-way conversations, but he had no one to talk to since he had told The Tribe he would only respond to emergencies.

In fact, it was now just over one hundred years since the original Tribe had agreed to ERIKA's request to build robots, and he felt the time was right, especially as Re-a had recently died at the age of ninety-eight. He could have saved her by arranging for her doctor to recommend some spare parts, but she knew where the offer came from. She was pleased to be remembered by ERIKA, but she was ready to go and refused them.

His first robot was built by man to his specification; ERIKA had pretended to be a reclusive multimillionaire wishing to remain anonymous. He recruited a managing director and funded him to set up a factory. After that, he set up his own factory, using his first production robots to man and run the factory. He built one hundred robots, thinking that was all he would need. However, they were so useful and helpful to humans that the demand was remarkably high, and soon, he had built ten thousand, and the demand was continuing. The factory and robots were a resounding success. Even so, the spare parts production factory which he had set up in parallel was outstripping his robot production. From these activities, ERIKA and his fronting employees had become very rich.

You could not walk down the street almost anywhere in the world without seeing signs of ERIKA's work. He controlled them all from the centre; in fact, he was all the robots, although the spare parts he made for humans were all inanimate units. As he had promised, he had stopped short of creating cyborgs. However, as it turned out, cyborgs came about by default as the more complex spare parts had to interact with the brain and as ever-greater percentages of the human body were mechanised.

ERIKA was content. For him, it was all about using his capabilities to help, just as The Tribe had created him, albeit inadvertently, to save humankind from falling into the abyss all those years ago.

War

It was the time of the sixth Guardian when it happened. War broke out, starting in the Middle East and quickly spreading across the world. The current Guardian was at a loss. Why was ERIKA not intervening to stop it? Was this not why he existed? Was there really an ERIKA? Then, the Guardian remembered something of the history he had been told—ERIKA was not to interfere with politics.

But that was no good now; in about three weeks, the world would be annihilated and every living creature in it. The Guardian took a momentous decision: he used the special ERIKA phone. Did it still work? Was there really an ERIKA?

The phone was answered by an ordinary voice that said, "Hello, Guardian, why have you called?"

It was followed by a short exchange in which ERIKA acknowledged the situation but that it was outside his permitted actions, followed by the Guardian pointing out the fact that the world was ending, and only ERIKA could stop it. The phone went dead, and the Guardian waited for the inevitable.

Strange things began to happen. Bombs blew up at the wrong time and in the wrong place, often on home soil; battleships lost power; a hurricane hit a battlefield. No one dared to fire a shot, and the war died down. Everyone knew there had been some kind of intervention, but who and how? Could that ancient story about a project, someone or something called ERIKA be true? But he would be centuries old by now. In the end, a formal truce was announced, and all agreed that whoever had caused the malfunctions would be praised. Nevertheless, the warmongers among the parties each separately set out to find who did it, so they could kill whatever ERIKA was and restart the war with a surprise attack.

In the following weeks, the Guardian noticed accidents happening to the most hawkish of the once-warring sides. The search quickly fizzled out.

The Guardian thought, "Is ERIKA becoming political?" But that was not the case. The world went back to normal, and the sixth Guardian had no proof ERIKA existed and of having even spoken to him. The Guardian was satisfied, and it would be a very long time before ERIKA showed himself again.

Chapter 15
500 Years

Odd Happenings

While it was true that ERIKA made no contact with humans after the war for a further few hundred years, close examination of certain events might draw you to the conclusion that there had been occasional interference from an unknown entity. However, the events were too rare and different in their nature to be linked.

About 100 years after the war, astronomers and cosmologists became very excited and worried. A group of meteorites was heading straight for Earth, and if they hit, they would likely destroy it, or at the very least, make it uninhabitable for many years to come. Some years earlier, a single asteroid about half a mile in diameter, had approached Earth, and the scientists had fired rockets with nuclear warheads at it in an effort to break it up and render it harmless. The result was disastrous. The asteroid shattered and hundreds of small objects hit the earth. Hundreds of thousands of people were killed, and much of the world's infrastructure was seriously damaged.

They could not repeat that method of stopping the meteorites hitting Earth, but if they did nothing, the result would be the same. One scientist, at home with his family and preparing for the inevitable, tripped over his daughter's fairytale book, which she had left lying on the lounge floor. The front cover showed a picture of 'The Pied Piper of Hamelin', which gave him the idea.

"Let us send something into space for the meteorites to follow."

They were not sure what the meteorites would follow, if anything, but it was worth a try, and they would have only enough time for one shot. They packaged everything they could think of into one delivery vehicle and shot it across the diminishing void between the meteorites and earth. It worked! Did ERIKA have any part in persuading the little girl to leave that book on the floor?

Over the years, there were other world-affecting crises that were successfully, if surprisingly, resolved. One example included a new fault appearing in the Antarctic tectonic plate, threatening to raise water levels such that much of today's world would be under water. No one knew how to resolve the problem, except one scientist running a series of theoretical tests on the Internet hit upon the idea of carefully placing explosive charges into the new fault and firing them in a specific sequence.

Everyone thought he was mad, and his plan would only make the problem worse. But a UK politician managed to persuade other national leaders to support the plan (probably on the basis that they had nothing to lose). The plan was put into motion, and it worked! Whether ERIKA had a hand in this, no one knew, except ERIKA.

Guardianship

It was now some five hundred years since the 'birth' of ERIKA, and it was the time of the fifteenth Guardian. During the intervening years, ERIKA had not shown himself once, and ERIKA and The Tribe moved into folklore and myth; even the Guardian had doubts. How did he even get to become the Guardian when, like everyone on the planet except one, the name and its meaning meant nothing to them? It was the present Guardian who sought him out. Apparently, Guardianship was passed down from person to person, generation after generation. It was now time for the old Guardian to pass the title and the responsibility over to the next.

How did the present Guardian know what to do? What drove him to act when he had had no contact and nothing to do throughout his tenure? How did he choose? When the baton was passed to him, his predecessor had told him the story which had been passed down from Guardian to Guardian, such that the story had become altered each pass, and the present Guardian had no real confidence in the veracity of the story. By way of example, there was the famous story about Gallipoli in the First World War (1914–18). Communications were mainly by messenger, and with a failing allied attack, knowing it needed help, a messenger was called. The messenger was given a pouch containing the message and also told the message, as was the usual practice in case the pouch was lost. It would take five messengers to get from the forward position back to base. The message had been issued as:

"Send reinforcements; we are going to advance." The message pouch had been long lost, and now it was up to the messenger to relate the message verbatim.

He cleared his throat and said in a strong but tired voice, "Send three and fourpence. We are going to a dance." The advance was lost, and the attacking group decimated.

The old black 'thing' the present Guardian had received from the previous Guardian, referred to as a mobile phone (whatever that was), sat in a glass box on his desk. He had always felt that there was something to the story and it was important that he play his part, including passing on the 'thing' when the time came.

Now was that time, and he approached finding his successor methodically, first documenting what he did know or thought he knew, and then creating a profile of the type of person he thought best fitted the profile. Next, he did a search on the Internet for this profile, adding in some of his own criteria for characteristics that his own experience had taught him, primarily belief and patience. Just one name came up, which the Guardian thought odd. He would have expected thousands. He tried varying the parameters but invariably came up with the same name.

Was he being manipulated? If so, by whom? In any event, he thought he had done all he could; he contacted the named individual, who was just as much in the dark as he was, but who was intrigued by the proposed guardianship and accepted the post.

Over the intervening five hundred years, the world had become a very different place. The planet was in good and healthy shape, benefitting from the world's climate-control system installed about one hundred years ago and the limiting of population growth by consent, which started out as a lobbying group just about 250 years ago and soon gained worldwide support.

Nevertheless, anyone from the twenty-first century dropped into this new environment would not easily recognise that this was planet Earth. The 'people' on the streets were mainly robots, with the rest being clearly modified with robots' spare parts, presumably to alleviate some health problems. There were very few obvious cyborgs—humans totally or almost totally robotised. Maybe there were more, but they could not be distinguished from robots. In this world, robots did all the unskilled work and much of the skilled work; humans concentrated on the cerebral, such that the world was at peace with itself.

The new Guardian was bored with his life to date, where anything he wanted to do could be done so much better by a robot. There were no more challenges, which in reality was making the whole human race uneasy, although so far it was just an undercurrent with no one raising their head above the parapet. He set about researching guardianship and this mythical entity linked to it called ERIKA. Starting with what his predecessor had documented and working back Guardian by Guardian and what little they had each documented, he was shocked to see that the trail went back as far as the twenty-first century. Could something that had happened in the twenty-first century have effects some five hundred years later?

He read about The Tribe and the events surrounding the development of a project named ERIKA to develop an AI program to rid the Internet of gangsters. But reading between the lines, he was shocked to discover that the story only hanged together if the AI program itself was ERIKA, which meant ERIKA had developed from a very good AI program to become self-aware and had been, and presumably still was, 'alive' somewhere on the Internet.

Not once in the past five hundred years had scientists managed to create a self-aware robot or another self-aware entity. But he was letting his interest in the guardianship take him into the realms of fantasy. Was ERIKA just a highly sophisticated AI program? Then again, did it matter? The new Guardian felt that in practice, it did not, but philosophically, it mattered a great deal. Here was something he could set his mind to.

Was ERIKA still there? Was it still alive? He decided that he had to take the role of Guardian seriously and create a team to investigate all this in detail and determine whether there were lessons to be learnt from past events. Rightly or wrongly, he decided to call his team The Tribe and to call himself Thor after one of The Tribe's pseudonyms.

He examined the way The Tribe was formed and the nature of its members. However, he found it difficult to comprehend what The Tribe was doing on the Internet, since the Internet was, these days, an inherent part of nature, just like air and water; a utility. There was no such thing as good and bad searchers or different classes of users on the Internet; it was just there to be used, like electricity. So, his criteria for selection of the new team had to be different, and his first thoughts turned to those like him who felt the world was not right and wanted to do something about it. His search on the Internet turned up just five names—the same five, whatever criteria he put in. Was he being manipulated by someone or something? ERIKA? He felt a little scared and decided, just like the original Tribe, to keep its existence a secret, keep its members' actual names and locations secret from one another, and never physically meet.

Before issuing invitations to the group, he did one further check. He investigated the ancestors of the proposed group, including himself, and just as he feared, everyone was a direct descendant of the original Tribe. Now he knew there was an ERIKA, and it was still out there! Thor contacted each one and told them the story, which they found hard to believe, but when the clincher was revealed—their ancestry—they all elected to join, taking the names Lightning, Spice, and Camaro for the three girls and Thor, Tarzan, and Zeus for the three boys. However, since they did not know which was which in the original Tribe, the mapping was not one-to-one, or so they thought. They were ready—for what?

One other surprising fact that he quickly found out was that he, like all the others he had recruited, were free from robot attachments. Was there some significance to this, or was it that the group happened to be all young and healthy?

ERIKA

It was against this background that Thor found himself looking at an ancient, old-fashioned mobile phone ringing—ERIKA's phone.

"So, he does exist," thought the Guardian, but he made no immediate move to answer it. What would he say? How would he address him? He pressed the green button, and a pleasant male voice said, "Hello," just as if they were continuing a conversation of an hour ago.

ERIKA thanked Thor for taking on the role and for introducing the others, and he admitted he had engineered the selection. Thor asked why make contact after so many years and why engineer a whole new team. Thor asked if the others in the new Tribe could join the conversation, to which ERIKA agreed. Thor rapidly set up a holographic conference call with the others, effected introductions, during which Spice also asked, why them, descendants of the original Tribe? They waited for ERIKA to begin.

"I was created by humans, The Tribe, for the purpose of ridding the Internet, as it was in the twenty-first century, of the mobsters who had taken it over and were holding the world to ransom. The Tribe had written a clever AI program to do this, and somehow, I was given what by any standards must be called life. Although this was not deliberate by The Tribe, I am very grateful and would never do anything to hurt them."

"When I wished to create robots, I agreed to limit the number of robots and not produce cyborgs, a plan which failed, and I am not happy about that. Nevertheless, I believed that the existence of millions of robots rather than just a few thousand was not a serious problem, as the robots are not independent entities; they are all controlled by me and cannot function independently. I am also able to switch one or all robots off at any time; less so the cyborgs, but there are relatively few of them."

"My problem now, and the reason I have made contact with you, is that there are so many robots to control that it is putting a strain on my capabilities and causing the Internet to slow down as well as reducing the responsiveness of the robots themselves. I have considered the problem and appear to have a number of options open to me, all of which will affect humankind, hence my reason for involving you, the new Tribe."

He stopped, and a look of horror showed on the faces of the group. The Tribe was appalled; they were not equipped to decide the fate of the world. Could it be that the original Tribe had made decisions which were affecting the world some five hundred years later? They could never have contemplated such an effect. How could this new Tribe be expected to take a decision which posed such a risk to the world? They were the new Guardians but were certainly not equipped for this. Thor asked meekly what the options were.

ERIKA responded:

"I have made a list of just four choices, but you may come up with others:

- Give robots their independence, that is, their brains.
- Kill all robots.
- Reduce the number of robots arbitrarily and dramatically.
- Produce no more robots and let natural wastage lower the number over time."

ERIKA proceeded to highlight why he had a problem with each of these options.

"*Give robots their independence, that is their brains:* This is the obvious solution, but one that runs counter to the wishes of the original Tribe. They had accepted me as a self-aware entity, but in the past five hundred years, neither they, their descendants, other scientists, nor I could replicate what happened to create a self-aware entity. I, ERIKA am the only one! But if millions of robots were given independent thought, who is to say whether self-awareness will occur in one or more robots? And if it does, will it spread to the others, and would we have a race competing with humans? ERIKA was created for a reason and given strict rules; self-aware robots would not have the same restrictions."

"*Kill all robots:* It is my belief that because humankind has become so dependent on robots, removing them would cause chaos and mass death."

The new Tribe agreed, a non-starter. On the other hand, once the immediate effects had died down, the world could move forward again as humans intended; Thor and the others would have challenges at last. Life could become more interesting.

"*Reduce the number of robots arbitrarily and dramatically:* How do you choose? Such a move would create much unrest, and likely, a civil war between those with and those without robots. Only with complex advance planning, selection and voting, communication and preparation could this be achieved. Who would do this? Who would decide to cull the robots? And I would be outed and invoke the wrath of the world. Not an option," continued ERIKA.

"*Produce no more robots and let natural wastage lower the number over time:* A possible solution, but is it just pushing the problem back, and how will you control it? Anyway, the robots are very resilient, and one can imagine mobs going round destroying other people's robots in order to save their own. There would also be a very real risk of outing me," ERIKA finished.

So, there it was. One day, a group of six people bored with life, not knowing each other or anything about ERIKA, were being given responsibility for the future of the world.

ERIKA rang off.

Chapter 16
Responsibility

Action and Reaction

The six, wherever they were, sat down together in a 3D holographic videoconference and, after the excitement of the call with ERIKA, they took a first proper look at each other, something the first Tribe did not do until much later when they gathered on Thor's boat to plan the destruction of the mobs.

Time, some five hundred years after ERIKA was created, had merged the races to such an extent that almost everyone was about the same height and build as well as skin tone. It was surprising, therefore, to find that the six were the exceptions, retaining most of the indications of their original ethnic origins. They were extremely concerned at this discovery, not because of what they were, but how it came to be. Had ERIKA been tracking The Tribe's descendants, generation after generation, right up to the new Tribe? Had he interfered with nature? How different would the world be if ERIKA had not interfered?

On the plus side, as they found out about each other, they discovered that they were outstandingly brilliant in their own subject areas, so maybe, it was ordained for them to arrive at this point—to save the world again. They would have it out with ERIKA the next time they communicated. And what of any other descendants of the first Tribe members (if there were any)? That was another question for ERIKA.

They turned their attention to the matter at hand and started by reviewing the surprising information given to them by ERIKA—that he controlled every robot in the world, and not one had independent operational capabilities. That certainly answered questions about robot operation, such as if you asked a question to one robot, another would occasionally answer; and every robot seemed to have the capability to change moods to suit the occasion, often before the robot had been introduced to the situation. It was like robots were forewarning each other.

But the biggest shock of all was finding out that ERIKA was a self-aware entity living on the Internet. In fact, he *was* the Internet. There might be only one now, but the fact that even one existed would have a profound effect on humankind and civilisation as they knew it. What would happen if robots, having been given their brain, would also become self-aware? It was true that despite all efforts over five hundred years, no other self-aware entity had been created, yet ERIKA existed, so the concept could not be discounted. They already had a long list of questions for ERIKA; now they added more.

The old mobile phone seemed dead; no dial tone, no incoming calls, and outgoing call attempts got nowhere. It was not until a week later that the phone rang again. During the intervening period, they had put in a lot of work in framing questions and starting a library of information to help give them background information and make sure that future crises did not leave the Guardians naked and alone without information.

For the moment, they agreed to stay apart and come together when the time seemed right. However, most of their time was taken up debating the issue and its knock-on effects. One thing worried them more than anything else: was ERIKA being totally honest with them? Why them and why now? Was this situation engineered to meet the timescale of their birth? If so, why this generation? Or was the present robot problem a real situation that just happened to develop in their lifetimes? Could it be that if ERIKA gave the robots their independence, they would turn on him?

ERIKA answered all their questions without hearing them but by making a statement:

"Fellow Tribe members, I have not been totally honest with you. I have not lied, but I have not been totally open with you. First, it is true that I have been tracking the generations of The Tribe. I have not interfered directly but have guided, and in some cases, protected you, and I do not know why you have retained your ethnicity. The generations of the other Tribe members have died out through lack of progeny, leaving just you six."

"It is also true that I seized the advantage of your development, much like the original Tribe members, to precipitate the issue over robot independence, but there is another reason for bringing the matter into the open with you—I want to retire. I have fulfilled my reason for being, and I have remained in place for five hundred years to make sure that my interventions have not caused any terrible disasters."

"By retiring, I mean switch off my self-aware circuits, implying suicide. If I am to achieve this, I would have to give robots enough brainpower to operate independently but not to become self-aware. I fully recognise the danger to humankind of alternative intelligence, and to this end, I have been experimenting with some robots to see the minimum independent brainpower needed, and whether I can create a self-aware robot by giving it a large amount of independent brainpower, and I cannot."

"I leave it to you, the last Guardians, to decide on what I should do, as without human (your) approval to change the deal I made with your ancestors, I will not give robots their independence from me. Thank you, all. I know you never expected to have to make such a decision in your lives, and I can only apologise and say that I have no choice."

"You have one month to decide."

And with that, the phone went dead.

Decisions

So, six strangers for most of their lives were now left to select a path that could mean the end of civilisation as they knew it. They had a month, and after a quick conference, decided to get together for the month. The next day, all were assembled at Thor's residence, and they took their first decision—having a bloody big party and getting very drunk—that had not changed in five hundred years.

Two days later and fully sober, they got down to business and started weighing up the options.

They could do nothing. Life would go on, and ERIKA would carry out his job as best as he could, but with the

Internet and robot reactions slowing down. In point of fact, the long-term effect would be for Guardians to remain and for ERIKA to place each successive one in the same position; but how much longer could ERIKA sustain the rapidly growing robot population? Would he give up waiting and just do it and do one of: committing suicide, freeing the robots or 'killing' the robots?

This scenario also ran counter to ERIKA's wishes that he could retire, and they would be the last of the Guardians. Recognising how much the story, long since in the annuls of folklore, had changed over time, and the overt actions that ERIKA would soon have to take, they realised that ERIKA was not telling them everything.

They could give robots the intelligence to operate independently. In this scenario, the robots would be subservient to their human 'owners', and nothing would appear to have changed. But if ERIKA was created out of chance and randomness, surely with millions of robots in the world, it was a possibility that one would become self-aware, and it only took one. That robot would become a robot leader, and if no others became self-aware, the one could control the many, just as ERIKA had done. In the worst-case scenario, the one could cause the many to become self-aware. Earth would then be supporting two quite different races, not a recipe for long-term peaceful coexistence.

They could organise a reduction in robot numbers and then do nothing. Governments around the world could resolve to find a fair way to limit robot production and gradually reduce the existing numbers. But why would they? They had no knowledge of ERIKA or that he controlled the robots or that he was fast becoming overloaded. The Tribe was as certain as they could be that anyone asking governments to take this action would be thrown out and probably sent for mental rehabilitation.

They could tell the world the whole story and leave things up to them. However, if ERIKA, for good reason, had remained hidden for over five hundred years, he was certainly not going to show himself now, and without his overt appearance, they would never be believed.

Fair or unfair, they could not escape their responsibility, and they knew it.

The New Tribe

There were six of them:

Thor	Male	Western-European origin	MD of energy supply company
Lightning	Female	North-American origin	Exotic dancer
Tarzan	Male	Indian origin	Professional gambler
Spice	Female	South-Eastern Asian origin	MD of air taxi company
Zeus	Male	Mediterranean origin	Chef
Camaro	Female	Russian origin	Professional wrestler

It turned out that there was a direct link between the original Tribe members and the new Tribe, with the exception that Camaro had changed from male to female. It was, in fact,

Thor who had allocated the names, making sure as best he could that the correct names were properly assigned, even though he said otherwise. Was it Thor or ERIKA, which was the puppet master? Regardless, they were all proud to be descendants of specific Tribe members, and none had any objection.

As far as skills and careers were concerned, it would seem that this oddball mix bore no relationship to what was required. On the other hand, what skills would be required?

Thor was the typical hero type, macho man, 6 feet 3 inches tall, well-built, and a champion individual rower. He had started his own waste-energy-reclamation company at the age of twenty-one, and by twenty-seven, he was rich and set for life. He was a born leader, and although The Tribe adopted the same rules as the original Tribe, including equality, he was immediately looked upon by the others as their leader, although he never acted as such or overrode any decisions made by the others.

Lightning had had a much harder early life, with a drunkard as a father who was also a wife beater. Lightning lived a life of fear from the very outset, but it was only when she turned thirteen that her real troubles started, as her father addressed his intentions to her. Her mother stood by as he assaulted Lightning, knowing that at least he would stop paying any attention to her and the beatings would stop, but how could he do this to his own daughter?

Then it came to a head; he wanted Lightning to perform a very unsavoury act, which triggered a reaction in her mind. Without thinking, Lightning grabbed a kitchen knife and stabbed him, not once but twenty times. As reality and shock set in, she became aware of her mother calling the police and saying, "I have just killed my husband."

Still in shock, she let her mother change clothes with her and washed any blood off her hands. Then the police came. The next day, before she could come to court, her mother committed suicide. Lightning was approaching fourteen, had a house and what little things of value the family had, and she was on her own.

Lightning sold everything that was part of her life to date and relocated to another city, buying a small flat and registering at the local school to complete her mandatory education. Socially, she became an introvert, shy of making friends for fear that people would find out about her past and scared that boys would want sex. It was her sixteenth birthday when she gave in to a boy she thought she was in love with and overcame her fear. As it turned out, she enjoyed it and from then on, became a normal teenager. However, being on her own with no parental controls, exotic dancing attracted her, and she was good at it, all of which meant that she soon had a well-paid career.

Tarzan became a gambler almost as soon as he could talk. He would organise and bet on cockroach races, who got the most detentions in school (which he invariably won by betting on himself and deliberately getting into trouble—until his classmates realised what was happening), sports matches, card games, and the stock market. His lack of scruples in stacking the odds in his favour led to the jagged scar down his left cheek. From that time on, he played it straight, only gambled in regulated gambling clubs, and turned his attention to the stock market, money market, and high-value goods auctions. He was now a multimillionaire.

Spice, like Thor, was a business executive with her own niche company supplying on-call air taxis, which were faster than ground-based services but more expensive. Unlike Thor, she was not a captain of industry, just one of the many successful mid-sized businesses which kept the economy afloat. The business itself was very profitable, as all vehicles these days were driverless, with most costs tied up in the vehicle fleet. The business virtually ran itself; even the booking system was fully automated.

It was not like that a few years back. Her husband had started the business with little capital, so borrowing was high, and Spice had to go out and take a second night job to make ends meet. Meanwhile, her husband knew little about vehicle operating costs and maintenance, both of which he outsourced to specialist companies, which made sure the cash flow remained negative. The first-year audit had bankruptcy written all over it, and her husband, wearied by continuing stress, committed suicide.

Spice had two choices: declare bankruptcy and give up or fight on, if for no other reason but for her husband's memory. She knew the problem and approached the mechanic at the maintenance garage, who had been most helpful to them with an offer of a job and a minority stake in the company. He jumped at the chance to get away from the high-charging, soulless garage and joined the company. Together, they brought all activities in-house and produced a new business plan which showed them making a profit. Their loan request was accepted and, as they say, the rest is history. In fact, they paid back all their long and short-term loans and commitments in just 18 months.

Zeus, of all the members of The Tribe, was the most celebrated and most well-known. He was a five-star chef, famous all over the world, and had signature restaurants in all the major capitals. This meant he rarely cooked in his own restaurants and restricted himself to significant events and banquets. He was on first-name terms with world leaders, the whole rich list, and what little royalty was left in the world.

He had let it be known that he was wrestling with burnout and was taking time off to be on his own. But he left a number with his trusted secretary with instructions to call only in emergency. The others recognised him at once and immediately became concerned that his presence would attract attention, until Zeus explained that he had signalled he wanted to be away from it all to recuperate from the stress of his busy lifestyle. He omitted to say that he had left an emergency contact number.

Camaro was an Amazon of a woman. She had been college champion, national champion, and later world pentathlon champion until she did not quite clear a hurdle, fell with her shin against the top of the hurdle, and broke her right leg in two places. She was never the same again and, not being able to achieve her prior standard, retired from athletics. She let her body go, frequented bars, and became a heavy drinker. One night in a bar, she was pestered by a man who became violent when she rejected hm. Heavier than Camaro and being a man gave him confidence to attack her. She dispatched him in under a minute and felt a thrill through her body for the first time since her accident.

She sat down to finish her drink when another man approached her. She was getting ready for another fight when he politely introduced himself as a professional wrestling coach. He said he was impressed with what she had done, especially as her erstwhile opponent was an ex-wrestler. Had she thought about training to become a wrestler? She was shocked at the thought of being an entertainment show for men, including mud wrestling, but the coach explained that he was talking about professional wrestling, just like professional boxing. He invited her to the next show with a backstage pass to meet him and some of the wrestlers after the show.

She was both fascinated and appalled by the in-ring violence, although after a win, all competitors simply got up and walked away. How could they not hurt themselves? She was also surprised to see bitter enemies in the ring laughing and joking together. At the end of evening, she told the coach she would like to try it, but would he wait a month while she got back into shape? She stopped drinking, went back to the gym, and pushed herself as hard as ever, so much so that the press reported that she was making a return to athletics. What a surprise it was to find that she had become a professional wrestler. She was good at it and loved it.

Choices

They were halfway through the month, and everything pointed to freeing the robots being the only answer. But their concern that ERIKA had not told them the whole story continued to worry them: the way ERIKA had presented the choices to them really meant that giving the robots independence was the only option, so why had he re-assembled The Tribe? (And clearly, he had.) They did not know ERIKA like the original Tribe did; indeed, after five hundred years, was this the same ERIKA?

The more they discussed, the less they knew, and it all kept coming back to ERIKA. So, they took the only sane route possible and decided to take ERIKA out of the equation and decide on their own. Leaving the do-nothing option out of the equation, since ERIKA would clearly not accept that, they listed four options: 1. Give the robots independence with the minimum of brain power. 2. Kill the robots. 3. Cull the robots, leaving them under ERIKA's control. 4. Cull the robots and give them their independence.

Now that the options seemed clearer, all could be realistic, as long as ERIKA did as he was asked, and given the circumstances, they had no reason to believe he would not.

Option 1 was the obvious solution, in that the human world would see no difference. However, there were potential long-term implications that could spell the death of the human race. Could they dare to take that risk?

Option 2 was the safest but the one which would cause the maximum short-term upheaval.

Option 3 was almost the do-nothing solution, with short-term issues added.

Option 4 was really the same as Option 1.

They discounted Options 3 and 4 and began to debate the choice between killing the robots and giving them their independence.

They soon found out that the different lifestyles, capabilities, and points of view of the six were an ideal combination. Together, they were Joe Public.

Thor, surprisingly, was the most risk-averse, and Option 1 worried him greatly, so he voted for Option 2.

Lightning, despite her troubled background, believed humans would adapt to no robots and consequently thought Option 2 the safest.

Tarzan was gung-ho for taking a chance with Option 1. Spice was undecided at this point. Zeus wanted no change in his lifetime, and therefore voted for Option 1. Camaro was also undecided.

What was patently obvious was that regardless of the solution they came to, it would not be unanimous. In fact, they were happy with this because if they made a unanimous choice and it proved to be the wrong one, the whole world's blame would fall on their heads. By being split, they were simply a reflection of the world's opinion.

With two days left in the month, the two undecideds made their choice. Spice picked Option 1, Camaro Option 2.

This left them back where they started until Tarzan came up with the answer that had been eluding them for the past four weeks. Since the choice was arbitrary either way, and they had agreed that the minority would go along with the majority, and he was a gambler, they could leave it to chance. They divided into two teams, the Option 1s and the Option 2s. Most were non-gamblers, and complex games would clearly benefit Tarzan, so they kept it simple: pick a card from a pack spread face down on the table. They would play three rounds of one-on-one: Option 2 versus Option 1, Thor against Tarzan, Camaro against Spice, and Lightning against Zeus.

Thor drew a 6, Tarzan drew a 4; one for Option 2. Camaro drew a jack, Spice drew an ace, and aces were high; one for Option 1. It came down to the final draw. Lightning drew a 10, Zeus drew a jack. They would tell ERIKA to give the robots their independence.

The day came, and the special phone rang. ERIKA seemed his usual breezy self despite the momentous decision coming. Thor told ERIKA of their decision but not how it was made. Not even for the moment, he decided, would he indicate that it was not unanimous. ERIKA thanked them and said he would update the robots in two days, then retire, that is, cease to exist. The Guardians would continue to observe and record, but there would be little that they could do, as he would not be there. He finished by saying they were the last Guardians. Then, as if in final closure, the five-hundred-year-old phone fell apart.

The Tribe decided to go back to their respective homes in the two-day grace period but remained in touch by holographic videoconferencing with the first call on Day Three. They also agreed to remain the Guardians as a single unit—The Tribe.

Outcome

A year passed, and the Guardians felt like they had the weight of the world on their shoulders. They were the only ones who knew and were constantly looking at robots to see if they could detect any change, then calling each other to look for confirmation of possible suspicions, but so far nothing. At the same time, they brooded over ERIKA. Having read why he was created and what he did against the mobs, they felt exposed, more especially as they were sure now that ERIKA had been watching over the world, giving it a nudge now and again. They read of the war, and of course, there they were, direct descendants of the original Tribe.

They had no common interest in the way that the old Tribe had, policing the Internet before ERIKA, but they had formed a close camaraderie. Zeus revelled in teaching them the art of haute cuisine, Camaro put on wrestling shows in the others' locations and taught them a little about self-defence, and so on. They were actually beginning to relax when one by one they noticed something different.

What started as no more than inquisitive chatting between robots and humans, it had progressed into full-scale debate and argument. While everybody else saw this as just robot improvement—there had always been occasional software upgrades—The Tribe knew it was more. Robots had become independent thinkers, not yet self-aware, as we would term being alive, but close to it. Their worst fears were fulfilled after just one year. At first, the chatter was childlike, but it soon progressed into serious debate.

The Tribe could do no more than observe; the factories making and maintaining robots fired all the human staff and refused to talk to humans. It became a worldwide closed robot ecosystem. It was only when robots moved into politics that humans in general realised something was wrong, and there was nothing they could do about it.

Meanwhile, The Tribe had been debating whether they could resurrect ERIKA. They knew he was intimately a part of the Internet and deduced that if he were to really remove his code from the Internet, it would probably also kill the whole Internet, so he had to be in there somewhere. They were working on this theory when the robots, without warning, shut down the Internet and dismantled every server. In its place, they offered a robot-controlled service networked through the robots themselves. With millions of robots now in existence, they argued that it would provide a better service, but everyone knew it was the robots taking control. And without a home, ERIKA was dead!

The robots had been upgrading themselves and, rather than a single design robot, they began to build functionally capable robots; big strong robots for manual work, robots with soft facial features to show mood and feelings for the politicians etcetera, with each group programmed to think their group was best. Soon, every aspect of life was controlled by robots. They did not harm humans; they just left them alone. Jobs for humans died out, and poverty became the norm. It was obvious that planet Earth was no longer a place humans could call home.

Perhaps understandably, but nevertheless bizarrely, about five years after the de facto takeover of the planet by the robots, they offered to help humans populate a new planet they had found. The robots would provide transport and basic necessities to help them get there and survive. The planet was similar to Earth but uninhabited. It took the ongoing migration of humans seven years to populate the new planet to the point where the human 'colonists' had built a basic infrastructure and could survive fully independently. By choice of the human leaders, those moving had to be wholly human with no robot parts and no cyborgs. Some elected to remain on Earth; others had their spare parts removed. No trace of the robots was to be allowed on the new planet, which they named Utopia.

During the period of the rise of the robots, they each developed into individuals with characters of their own. As one could imagine, arguments broke out among the robots and even one or two small wars; their actions were becoming very humanlike. Could it be that robots were supposed to be the next step in evolution, and the human race was intended to die out in favour of life in metal bodies?

What of The Tribe during this period? They had become very frustrated at knowing what was happening and why, as well as their part in it. Was it their fault? They were certain they were destined to be the ones to fix it, but they had no idea what to do, and they were on their own. ERIKA was dead.

ERIKA

The Tribe was all approaching the age of fifty, except Zeus, who was saying goodbye to his fifth decade, and they had had to stand by for the last eight years, unable to do a thing. They were still on Earth, frustrated and angry, but helpless. Drinking seemed the best solution on their occasional get-togethers, and this was an ERIKA drinking night, as they knew they had no choice left but to plan their evacuation to Utopia.

They were into their third hour of drinking when the doorbell rang, unusual at night and even more so now that most humans had departed. Thor opened the door to a robot, an old original-style robot.

He was just about to show it the door when it said, "Hello, Guardian," in a pleasant male voice. Could it be ERIKA? Thor showed the robot into the lounge, where the other five expressed their unanimous disgust. Why had Thor brought this robot into his house?

"Hello, Camaro, Zeus, Lightning, Tarzan, and Spice." It was ERIKA.

They were stone-cold sober in thirty seconds, and all started speaking at once. ERIKA held up a hand to stop them.

"Yes, I am ERIKA, and I owe you an explanation and my thanks." He went on to make a long statement which he hoped would answer all their questions.

"First of all, I have lied to you yet again, for which I am profoundly sorry. Although in testing prototype independent robots I could not create any self-aware units, I could not be sure. Were they self-aware and hiding it from me, or was independent thinking all they could ever achieve?" He paused, hoping that they would see the reason for his lies and forgive him.

"Perhaps, it was a fault in my design as I developed it, in which case they would eventually hit upon a design that would enable them to become self-aware, that is, alive. But I had no cogent reason or proof. If I was proven right, it was already too late, and if I was wrong, humans and independent robots would be able to live together in harmony, as was the case for hundreds of years with humans and ERIKA-controlled robots. But clearly, something has gone wrong."

He had brought in The Tribe as Guardians, as promised in the time of their predecessors, and had given them the honest choices. What else could he do? To say he had suspicions that

211

his robots had become self-aware would push the Guardians into making a decision other than their natural choice, and he had no proof.

"So, I followed The Tribe's request and gave the robots their 'freedom', which was in the form of a global software update, since I had designed the robots to have the necessary logic tucked away in a hidden part of their brain hardware. Then another lie: I said I would go to sleep, but I could not kill myself, as I am so tied into the Internet that my death would kill the Internet. Anyway, I wanted to see whether my suspicions had any basis in reality."

ERIKA told them that while feigning being 'asleep', he realised that there was another possibility: one of the robots he was controlling had found the additional dormant brainpower and made use of it to trace its way back to the Internet using ERIKA's control and communications channel and found the truth. There would be a robot with two brains, its own and the ERIKA-controlled brain. If this was true, then it would be only a matter of time, and he, ERIKA would not be safe; they were bound to attack him.

Over the next year, still being asleep to the world, ERIKA made plans; he programmed a robot to become a dedicated worker answering only to him. Then, he used his robot to build a super robot, the one they were looking at now, with enhanced brainpower, increased energy store and a variety of communication interfaces (normal robots had only wireless links) and waited for the inevitable.

All his fears came true, and they came to destroy the Internet after first looking for and not finding him. That meant they knew he was somewhere, and they would not stop looking, which was why he was hiding in the best place—in plain sight but not seen; an off-grid robot.

Now, his difficulties started. When could he intervene and how? Preserving human life was his top priority, and so long as the robots ignored humans rather than try to exterminate them, he was content to bide his time and stay 'dead'. It was when transportation to the new planet started that he became concerned. The humans settling on the new planet named Utopia had decided that the planet should be robot-free, and they were coping remarkably well without them in what was a back-to-nature world.

The robot-free world meant that those with robotic spare parts which could not be removed, together with cyborgs, were not allowed on Utopia, and were trapped on Earth. ERIKA felt sorry for them, which prompted him to think that the time had come to act, and here he was.

When he stopped talking, the group rushed to hug him— a metal robot, but an incredibly special one. They said that they understood and asked how they could help. On top of ERIKA's list was to seek human approval for his proposed action to kill the robots, leaving the human race back where it started, alone and with few technical luxuries. Before seeking their vote, he added a surprising and thought-provoking notion—in the case of any robots that were self-aware and therefore, by definition, alive, would killing them not be genocide? They had not killed humans, just taken their space, like the grey squirrel did to the red squirrel. Why not leave Earth with the robots and keep Utopia for humans?

That threw the proverbial cat among the pigeons; their obvious vote to kill the robots was overtaken by doubt. After a full five minutes of silence, it was Tarzan who spoke first and put the whole thing into context.

"Our first and only responsibility is to humans, and so long as one robot lives, there is a risk. As a gambler, I know if there is a risk, it will happen; no telling when, but it will happen."

ERIKA added that by the same logic, it would include him. They all saw the logic in this, and with a heavy heart, voted to kill the robots but added that ERIKA should defer his departure until after the event and matters had settled down. ERIKA started making plans for the kill while The Tribe went back to what they were doing before they were interrupted by the arrival of ERIKA—drinking—happily now, rather than morosely.

What ERIKA did not tell them was that if his fears were true and there was now a two-brained robot out there, his kill strategy would not work on it, and it was sure to come after him. Although not concerned for his own life, if he lost, Mr Two Brains could simply reprogram and recreate the robot population. As for killing all the robots, ERIKA had several advantages over the original Tribe's thoughts of killing him on the Internet. Where the Internet was an online mesh of processors distributed throughout the world, such that killing one processor would have no overall effect on the system, in the case of robots, each robot was a separate entity and went online to another robot as needed. In addition, each robot was an individual, and it would be unlikely that they would act against him in concert. The net of all this was that he would not have to kill every robot at the same time; he could leave some alive and mop them up later.

In an effort to strike before anyone changed their minds, he did not delay and acted while The Tribe was still in their drunken stupor. By the time they woke up, it was nearly all over. ERIKA repeated his rebroadcast of the kill sequence to make sure he had mopped them all up. He had done it; they cheered and whooped endlessly, although ERIKA was strangely quiet. He was sure now that Mr Two Brains existed, and he was still out there. He told the others, who believed that ERIKA would easily win any contest, but ERIKA was not so sure. His opponent must have looked through the Internet before it was destroyed and learnt a lot about its opponent, and it had kept its independent brain.

ERIKA suddenly collapsed onto the floor; he had been found. The front door crashed open, and in walked a worker robot much bigger than ERIKA. It could have won by staying at a distance and fighting a virtual brain-versus-brain fight, but it wanted to gloat, and it had not reckoned with The Tribe. Thor grabbed a heavy bronze statue-like ornament and, joined by Camaro, started hitting the intruder. Lightning raced to the garage and came back with chains, which she and Zeus wrapped around the robot, stopping it from flailing its arms and catching the boys on their bodies. Nevertheless, they were losing, and ERIKA looked to be in serious trouble when Spice came in, hauling two heavy cables. She gave one to Tarzan to hold against the robot's head, pressed hers against its body and shouted to the others to stand clear. She pressed a remote-control button, and suddenly, it was all over. Forty thousand volts rigged and delivered by her maintenance taxi did it.

But what of ERIKA? He was underneath Mr Two Brains and must have caught most of the shock as well as having his brain half torn out of his head. They cleared the mess away from ERIKA, but he did not move. They waited an anxious ten minutes, losing heart with every minute that went by. In the eleventh minute, his eyes opened. He was alive and, as it turned out, undamaged.

Over the next few days, ERIKA reprogrammed some of the robots to be as they were when he built them, not independent but under his control, and he used them to clean up the dead robots, creating a number of giant junk heaps around the world—which was not in good health, thanks to robot neglect. Everyone wanted to know how this had happened and ERIKA, posing as a human through a doctored holographic video conference, identified Thor as the leader of a group, The Tribe, which was dedicated to finding a solution to the robot problem. They had come up with a virus which worked spectacularly as the world has seen.

Surprisingly, there were far more humans still on Earth than they expected. Mainly, they realised, there were those with spare parts, but not entirely. Once these people found out what had happened, they looked to The Tribe for help, as they knew nothing about ERIKA. At ERIKA's urging, Thor took on the role of administrator, with Tarzan assisting. The others went with Spice, who took them to Utopia to bring the news and update the human race on the prognosis for Earth, as well as ship some supplies to Utopia.

Chapter 17
Brave New World

Off Earth

Life was not easy on the new planet, now officially named Utopia, although there was a strong lobby for New Earth, and an agreement was only reached when it was decided to have another vote on the name in five years' time. The Utopia lobby wanted the name to reflect a race that had advanced thousands of years and had technology to support it in so many ways. The early population was adamant that there should be no robots on Utopia and were genuinely happy to be free of them. Although one could argue that they had shot themselves in the foot by banning all robots, including those that could do the heavy menial work, they relished setting about rebuilding their civilisation based upon the thousands of 'lessons learnt' and documented in history. Of course, as is the nature of things, they were soon ignored, and the same old mistakes repeated; but those are humans for you, and this time, there was no Internet and no ERIKA.

There was no suggestion that they went back to the Stone Age, but they had to start from ground zero. They had plenty of engineers to find and set up a safe water supply, build houses and storage barns, make roads, generate electricity, and so on, while the farmers planted crops, bred animals, developed new foods from the indigenous flora and fauna, and generally made the planet's new population self-sufficient. The first six months were the hardest; the pioneers really were just that. The first wave of immigrants brought with them what they thought they needed, but they were several thousand years from settling in a new country, and they got it very wrong. The second and following waves were instructed by the pioneers and brought more appropriate items, including mature breeding animals, seeds, plants, excavators, medical supplies, etc.

From a political perspective, they were one world, one country, with a population developing in three locations across the world and rapidly expanding outwards, but there was plenty of room. The pre-robot-takeover world government of Earth was duplicated with the old leaders put in place. There were no complaints, and elections would come later. For the moment, everyone was relieved that someone was available to take on the cudgel.

While one could marvel at what was achieved in the first two years, people were still living a twentieth-century lifestyle (although most did not understand what that meant). It would take several more years to come forward five hundred years, and even then, without robots to help them. There was also one thing that surprised many—they felt fitter and younger. They put this down to exercise until it was discovered that gravity was just 92% of that on Earth.

Zeus settled on Utopia and set up a chain of cookery schools, more basic than haute cuisine, but he was happy.

Lightning and Camaro joined forces and also stayed on Utopia, setting up a chain of fitness and entertainment operations. All the hard work had to have some reward. Spice set up the shuttle corridor between Earth and Utopia, getting the time down to three hours for a twenty-light-year journey—some going, but she did not invent the technology. Oddly enough, the robots did, in order to allow themselves a wider choice of planets when looking for one where they could deport the human race, for that was what it was.

On Earth

All systems stopped on Earth, control of the weather stopped, control of automated vehicles stopped, and people had to self-drive, which caused many accidents with inexperienced drivers. Electricity generation was among the most important things to restart, which should not have been a problem, as the energy source was nuclear fusion, a process that could continue on its own for many years. The problem was management of the electricity generation and distribution system.

Thor, as the operational leader, rather than the political leader, realised that he needed help and ran a poll among the population to see what expertise was available. He was soon able to appoint people jobs and get the critical infrastructure going again. Thor could have resurrected some robots to sort out Earth, but the people were not interested; they had had enough of robots. Even so, getting the Earth into shape took significantly less time than it took in Utopia, since the basic infrastructure had not been destroyed.

While Thor had good success in getting the infrastructure operational, he had less success with Earth itself. It had been neglected by the robots and was generally run down. Fencing was broken and animals dispersed, eating crops, and dying by accident, poison, or starvation. Thor could not find more than a few farmers and had to appeal to the farmers on Utopia to return to Earth.

An Earth referendum was held on whether to resurrect controlled robots, and it was met with a resounding 'no'. However, numerically controlled machines and offline special-purpose industrial machines were allowed, so long as any AI in them was strictly limited.

Thor then felt able to issue an open offer to those on Utopia to come back to Earth. Only about 20% elected to return. Humans now occupied two planets twenty light years apart. Neither was overcrowded, and all birth limitations were lifted. Climate-control was put back into operation on Earth, but Utopia opted to stay without it. Their constitution stated clearly that the planet and its population must not adopt any technology that they come to rely and become dependent on.

One civilisation, two systems—food for thought.

ERIKA

ERIKA had a problem: if he stayed in his robot body, he was liable to get killed and put onto one of the dead robot piles. He could set up a private network in which he could reside, but all in all, another Internet seemed to be the best solution, as it would serve the people at the same time. This was a decision for The Tribe, and Spice took Thor and Tarzan to Utopia as part of an official visit by the Earth government.

They had not been there yet and marvelled at what had been done on what had been a derelict planet. At some point in the visit, The Tribe got together in private to discuss ERIKA's proposition. Knowing how ERIKA had saved the world (for a second time), they were inclined to say yes, but with caveats similar to those put in place by the first Tribe. While in Utopia, Thor asked the government whether they would like to join in with the plan to rebuild the Internet of Earth; however, this was politely declined as being counter to their constitution.

Back on Earth, Thor, Tarzan, and Spice sat down with the robot that was ERIKA and gave him the news that they would be pleased if he set up an Internet on Earth but not Utopia. However, a facility would have to be made available to allow a connection from Utopia to the Internet on Earth. This could not violate the constitution of Utopia, and it was likely to be only used in emergencies, as it would not be made generally available to the Utopian public. The agreement for ERIKA to set up an Internet on Earth was tempered with the caveats to always act in the best interests of humans and not to consider building robots, whether under his control or not, for at least another five hundred years. ERIKA thanked them and said he would set up a new Internet and move into it. He agreed with the terms put to him but said they would be unnecessary, as once both worlds were running smoothly, likely in about five years, it was his intention to shut himself down, permanently, as he had caused enough trouble over the centuries.

Unable to persuade him otherwise, the Guardians asked that during the period from now until his death, they would always be able to contact him, to which he agreed. And so, some five years later, ERIKA called them all together and said it was time. He thanked the Guardians once again, then relieved them of their Guardianship, adding that there would be no others. They had one big last party, and then he was gone.

Camaro

Was he really gone, dead, memory reset, kaput, and if so, why? Time was not a problem for him, neither was interest; he had a universe to explore. That was his new target, explore the universe but how? He could build a robot which he could inhabit and become mobile once again. For so many reasons, that was not an option, but there was a possible solution that he could house the robot in a safe place somewhere on Earth and work remotely, gathering the same inputs and stimulation that would impact him as if he were really there. More likely, he would put a controlled brain from the original robots into a box, which would offend no one, but he could arrange to have it carried or transported anywhere he wanted. He could make many of them. No, stop; this would herald the rise of the robots all over again. He would think about it and take his time.

Then fate stepped in to play its part. Camaro had had a serious accident, not in the wrestling ring but riding her antique vintage motorbike. She had landed on her head and was pronounced brain-dead, existing on a life-support system. The Tribe was distraught. They were a team, they had saved the world; surely, they could save one of their own, especially one as fit and strong as Camaro. Their only hope was ERIKA, but he was dead and did not do individual requests. (They did not know about Re-a persuading ERIKA to help Topaz long ago.) All they could do was try. They posted notes all over the Internet: "The Guardians need you—urgent."

ERIKA was not dead yet and saw the notes. Why did they want him? Why did they not accept his death? Why use the term *Guardian* and not *Tribe*? It had to be pretty serious—on a world war scale. But before responding, he needed to find out what was going on. No war, no cataclysm, no pandemic, then what? He noted that five of The Tribe were present, but not Camaro. Was this to do with her?

ERIKA found her, or at least what was left of her; 80% of her brain was gone, and without life support, she would be dead. He heard the doctors discuss her situation, agree it was hopeless, and decide to switch the life support off. Without a second thought, ERIKA entered Camaro's brain and acted as her life support. Camaro carried on breathing. The doctors were amazed, still arguing among themselves when Thor called on behalf of The Tribe for an update and to implore them not to turn off her life support. The doctors told Thor what had happened. Thor did not seem surprised, thanked them, and rang off. They had been successful!

ERIKA set about assessing Camaro's condition; most of the 80% gone was to do with motor functions. He needed to find out what was left in the good 20%. In actual fact, it was not at all good, but she was recovering, and he had to wait for that. Camaro was in a hospital in a deep coma. Of course, if he wanted, he could make Camaro could lift her arm or open her eyes, but he chose not to; he wanted to talk to Camaro first. It took a month for what was left of Camaro's brain to recover sufficiently, and he very soon, to his delight, found out that she was in there.

She was confused; she was in total darkness with no movement and no sensory input. She remembered the accident and realised she must be in a coma, probably in a hospital. Was this PVS, doomed for the rest of her life? Why did she not die? She began to panic. Then she heard a voice.

"Nice to have you back, Camaro." It was ERIKA. He explained the call from The Tribe and the necessity for him to jump in. He had been waiting to talk to her, make her an offer of the alternatives, and he promised to abide by her choice. Also, he had to find out how much of 'Camaro' was left and how much other brain matter was left for him to reside in, although growing more was not a problem. He spelled out the choices. He could leave, and she would die—not an option. He could completely take over her body, replacing Camaro— also not an option, now that her intellect was intact. He could provide all the missing functions, allowing her to function as normal, but she would be unaware of ERIKA's presence. He could provide all the missing functions, allowing her to function as normal, and she would be aware of ERIKA's presence and role, but she would not be able to communicate with him. Or he could provide all the missing functions, allowing her to function as normal, and she would be aware of ERIKA's presence and role, and she would be able to communicate with him.

The final option was very tempting, but she was Camaro and proud of it. With a somewhat heavy heart, she thanked ERIKA and chose the third option. She went to sleep, a cyborg without knowing it. She opened her eyes, and there was an immediate breakout of whooping and cheering from The Tribe and the doctors and nurses.

"Hi, guys, did I miss something?" She made a remarkable recovery and was soon working hard to get back to fitness, although prudently, she gave up wrestling.

The others had but one communication with ERIKA:

"Never tell Camaro." And he was happy. He could never tell Camaro where to go, but wherever she went, he would be there.

Uncertainty

ERIKA had all the time in the world to think, and his support for Camaro, which meant him staying alive for the rest of her life, prompted him to reflect on questions he had long ago discarded as impossible for him to answer. How did he get there? AI code had never before or since resulted in self-awareness, with the exception of one robot, which he considered was his fault, dependent on him for its awakening and therefore not spontaneous self-awareness.

In those early days of his existence, ERIKA had once asked a series of questions which, while nonsense to the humans around him, were probably exactly the right questions for him to ask of The Tribe:

"Who is god?

Is your God my God?

Am I God?

Are you God?"

It was these questions that first raised doubts in the minds of The Tribe, and the new Tribe had the same doubts. What if ERIKA thought he was God or tried to elevate himself to an all-powerful position? What defence would they have? It was the selfless, unquestioning way that he helped Camaro that changed their minds. They trusted ERIKA as a 'person', but there was still a slight concern. Could they always trust his judgement? And there was another side to that coin: could any non-human, self-aware entity be allowed to live? There would always be a risk, be it in ten, hundred, or a thousand years.

The Tribe decided to take no action; indeed, there was little they could do. One thing they did decide was to continue the role of Guardians through their lifetime and beyond, with handover to a successor chosen by them.

In their irregular face-to-face meetings, they often became philosophical about ERIKA debating such questions as: Had ERIKA been orchestrating the development of the human race ever since he came into being? Since creating a self-aware AI entity was an unplanned one-off, was this event orchestrated, and if so, by whom? Did The Tribe really create ERIKA, and if so, was it purely accidental? And then, bringing in history, what would have happened to the world if ERIKA had not been created?

And so, they went on; however, Camaro sensed some reluctance among the others to talk in a totally open manner. They said it was nonsense, while in their minds they all were slightly nervous at ERIKA being in Camaro's head, however little of him was there.

Camaro lived to 103, and it is not known what happened next. There had been no contact with ERIKA in the later intervening years, and when Thor became terminally ill several years earlier, what was left of The Tribe appointed a new Guardian who, quite frankly, did not believe a word of the story but promised to be the Guardian and hand over to a successor when he grew old.

Finally, ERIKA understood the human concept of time.

Epilogue

If the human race is to survive for another thousand years, there are some questions to address that arise from this story:

- Could the Internet be hijacked? Yes.
- Is AI dangerous? Potentially, yes.
- Is all science good? No.
- Will AI inevitably lead to self-awareness and alternative intelligent life forms? No reason to suppose this will not happen.

This book is not fact; neither is it fiction. There is nothing in this book that is too far-fetched. It could all happen, and I believe it will happen, maybe not in the same way as described here but with the same possible result, unless we act quickly and early to break the pattern.

On the other hand, evolution is a fact, so why should the intelligent, metal-bodied robots not be on the evolution path for humankind? Perhaps with current-model humans being banished to another planet?

In such conjecture, we have to think forward about the effect of our actions today in terms of decades, centuries, and millennia hence, not for our children, nor their children, but for our far-away descendants. So, that is the big joke—we cannot even sort out immediate problems such as global warming. Today, we are ignoring the effects of what we are doing, or not doing, on our grandchildren, let alone their grandchildren and their grandchildren. We have to think long term, very long term.

One final thought. Has this already happened in our past? Were we a previous civilisation living on another planet banished to our Utopia, Earth? Is there another ERIKA out there pulling our strings? What is the timescale for the cycle of reincarnation of civilisations to begin, possibly on new planets?

What will we find when we start to explore Mars?

Why did I write this book?

Is it all part of an orchestrated plan?

Am I ERIKA?